I LIKE MY WOMEN BBW

By Cole Hart

Chapter 1

After being away for almost a year, King walked out of Phillip's State Prison in North Georgia with so much swagger you would have thought he'd just won an NBA championship. He was feeling like a new man with a new life. Sniffing the air of freedom gave him a bolt of energy, even though this wasn't his first time getting out after facing multiple charges. His homies on the inside waved and shouted out their goodbyes, while a few female guards he'd had personal dealings with frowned upon his dismissal. King was the man inside and outside of those prison walls. He got pussy no matter where he was. Felicia, a night shift guard, begged for him to fuck her every other night. She would even bring in other female guards to watch him have sex with them. She would play with her pussy, letting King finish her off by bringing her to a climax that no other man had given her before. Everything about him made her panties wet. Her kitty cat purred at the sight of him and became a magnet, always finding his dick as if life depended on it. She was saddened the most, especially after having terminated the pregnancy that had derived from her and King's sinful actions. He didn't give two fucks about either of the prison broads though. They were fun girls that helped him pass time. But he wasn't interested in dealing with them in the free world. Nothing gave him greater joy than knowing that he was about to see the one woman who was embedded in his heart. That woman was Delishus Jones. She had a big heart, but an even bigger figure to uphold it. King had had women of all sizes in his lifetime. However, Delishus was the only one who weighed in at over 200 pounds. He loved how her thickness was curvy and yet still beautiful. A BBW, otherwise known as a Big Beautiful Woman, is what they called her type of women. Beautiful, Delishus was indeed. She'd kept him straight while he was in prison with cards, letters, Green Dots, phone calls, etc. In his eyes, she was the most official chick that he'd ever met. However, there was one issue in the way and that was his baby mama, Harmony.

Unfortunately, Harmony was waiting outside the gates instead of Delishus. He spotted her picking at her gel nails, anticipating his presence. King showed himself, still standing tall at six feet even, weighing roughly around one hundred and seventy pounds of all muscle, and having the physique. He'd become accustomed to when he first entered the boxing ring. Women flocked to him because of his intoxicating hazel eyes and good wavy hair. His skin was dark and smooth, his face was chiseled just perfect, and he had the prettiest white teeth that anyone had ever seen. Talking about a sexy thug fresh out of prison, every woman wanted to have a taste of his chocolate. A thick nigga like him came a dime a dozen out of the prison system around the world, but no man went as hard as King. The streets feared him and most competitors in the ring could see their ass whooping coming a mile away.

"Oh shit, there go my baby! King! Over here!" Harmony shouted, gaining his attention. He looked in her direction while every other female's head turned to stare at his fine ass. Harmony peered around the parking lot at women of different backgrounds who seemed to be waiting for their released loved ones, but somehow managed to have an eye for King. She dared one of them bitches to speak to him. Harmony might've sounded like a pretty girl, but she most definitely was not on the outside.

Her money was the only thing that made her attractive because she used it to buy expensive makeup, fake lashes, nice name brand clothes and keep her hair weave fly. She had the lips of a small fish and a face like "Sheneneh" from Martin Lawrence's television show. On the inside, she was just as ruthless as King when it came to her personality. If there was a reality show called *Real Hood Bitches Of Atlanta*, she'd be the number one star on there.

King observed her coke bottle figure that she never lost, no matter how many of his children she had. He had doubts about the kids being his, but he always kept that to himself. Sharing two kids with Harmony was a mistake. Twice she claimed to be on birth control pills, and twice she trapped him with unexpected pregnancies. That only raised his level of doubt. Being in a relationship with her for over five years had its ups and downs like any other relationship.

Harmony ran to King with opened arms, letting the other women know that she was his prize. He wrapped his muscular arms around her waist and kissed her glossy lips. They were just as plump as his and reminded him of how good her lips made his dick feel. Regardless of how people saw them as a power couple in public, he knew there was one woman he loved just as hard in private. She was the woman he couldn't wait to see and have near him.

And her name wasn't Harmony.

"Hey love, um um um. Damn you look good! I see you held things down for a playa and I 'preciate you," King said to her, walking up to their Lexus coupe. It really wasn't *theirs* because Harmony paid the note on it. He just pretty much drove it whenever his car was down. But just like always, King took over anything she owned and Harmony let him. She bought him any car he wanted. However, he always sold it and somehow ended up costing her more money in the long run. Claiming what's hers *is* his; he didn't hesitate to spend her money when she offered it.

Harmony's mother, Debra, ended up becoming wealthy when one of her late husbands suddenly died. It was rumored that Debra and Harmony fed him rat poison, yet stated that they didn't understand how he'd mysteriously become ill. To this day, no one questioned the autopsy report, so they were living large off of the more than two-million dollar insurance policy that was taken out on him. Because King lived with them, he found himself doing everything they asked, knowing that he didn't have anywhere else to go. His parents had died years ago and he didn't feel comfortable laying up on any of his other family members. It also helped that Harmony spent her money on him freely, buying fancy designer clothes and expensive jewelry, making sure he stayed fly.

"Thanks daddy. You're lookin' hella good too! Got these hoes out here 'bout to tip over, they're staring so hard!" she stated, then looked around and rolled her eyes and neck. Then she yelled, "What y'all hoes staring at? Yeah, I'm winning! What!" Harmony said, showing her true immature side by cutting her eyes at all four women. There was no such thing as a *perfect* woman, and Harmony was proof of that. She carried rude and cocky ways, reminding any man to never consider her as their "dream girl". She poked her tongue out, making the women snap back into reality and refocus on their reason for being outside of the penitentiary gates in the first place. "Yeah, that's what I thought. I'll shut this parking lot DOWN! Play with me if you want to," Harmony added.

"Bitch, get yo' childish ass in the car! Was all that even necessary?" King asked, shaking his head and slamming the door. It had been a while since he made contact with anyone other than his main bitches, Harmony and Delishus. He reached back and grabbed the backpack Harmony had brought to him and pulled out his Galaxy Note. He turned it on and waited for it to boot up.

"Yes it was! I gotta let these bitches know the deal. So, what we doin' today?" Harmony asked, over thrilled at his early release. She started the engine, gripped the steering wheel, smiling and thinking that her day couldn't get any better. A quick glance over to King changed her thoughts.

"Mmm hmm, I think you were being extra back there," he replied without taking his attention away from the phone, going straight to his Instagram page.

"God! I am so glad to have you back with me. The kids are driving me crazy asking about you, wondering when you were coming home. I know they can't wait to see you. Did you miss us?" she asked while grooving to Ashanti's "Foolish". After hearing no response, she became angry with him for ignoring her. "Yo, what you doin'? Who got you skinning and grinning?" Harmony asked abruptly. King was so into his phone he didn't even hear her questions. Being the chick Harmony was, she snatched his phone out of his hand to see what had his undivided attention. She looked at the face of the phone. The images and comments before her sent her into a rage.

"Shawty, gimme back my shit!" King demanded. His thick baritone voice was demanding but didn't stand a chance with her. She was used to his mischief, but expected different considering the time he'd been away from her. Every woman wants that one man that will appreciate her loyalty and show the same in return. King was far from loyal when it came to his love for women, particularly when it comes to Delishus.

"Who the fuck is 'Delishus'? And what you liking all this fat ass bitch's pictures for? Commenting on them and shit. You diggin' 'Precious' looking bitches now?" Harmony questioned in an uproar. *I know this nigga don't believe her fat ass is cute!* Even while driving reckless, she held her free hand up, preventing King from getting back his phone.

"Aye, stop playin'! I don't go through yo' phone, so show me the same respect! All I did was say that she looked nice," he argued. He was caught. His likes and comments under her selfies, as well as other personal photographs of the full-figured woman, proved he had a thing for *big* girls. King met Delishus a few months before he went to prison and it was love at first sight for him. She wrote to him religiously regarding the days they shared before he got locked up. He loved the fact that she wasn't ashamed to pour out her heart to him in ways he never imagined. His feelings for her matured and grew the more he got to know her. He couldn't wait to see her again and hated that he got arrested before they got a chance to enjoy each other one more time.

"Well take yo' damn phone back then!" Harmony yelled, pissed at his undermining her. She threw his phone hitting him in the chest with it. "Let me find out you fuckin' Miss Piggy and we gone have some *major* problems!"

"Whatever. Drop me off at the crib! I ain't 'bout to argue with you," King responded, hoping to drop the subject. He clicked off Delishus' IG profile page, went to Facebook and sent an inbox to a few of his homeboys, letting them know he was out and ready to discuss business.

"Hello!" Harmony answered her phone, still annoyed at King's actions. Mainly, since he returned to his online shenanigans. She slammed on the brakes causing his head to jerk forward and nearly hitting it on the dashboard, making his phone fly into the windshield. "Can you see better now? Got yo' damn attention in that phone too hard! Don't you come home and be giving my dick away to no other woman, you got me?" Harmony threatened, squeezing his genitals.

"Ouch! What the fuck?" King said while retrieving the phone and grabbing her wrist simultaneously. A sneak peek of the phone showed Harmony another picture of the same full-figured woman, yet it was in his phone showing as a contact photo.

"Get out! Since you want to talk to fat bitches, let them haul yo' ass around then!" Harmony shouted. She hit the unlock button to let him know that she was serious.

"Quit playing girl, that's my damn cousin! I haven't said anything freaky or nothing like that, so chill out. Take me home before I beat that ass and make you remember who I am!" King said, deepening his voice and putting emphasis on his threat.

"Whatever, you better not put yo' hands on me!" she said, slowly taking her foot off the brakes, but went heavy on the gas pedal, jerking off again into traffic. "Anyways, hello! Oh hey girl. Nothing just picked up my man... Yeah, you know he got out today... Um, let me check, hold up... Baby, you mind if I go out to chill with the girls tomorrow night?" she asked, now acting as if she hadn't just clowned on him.

"I don't give a damn what you do," King told her, still pissed at her childish ways. He bit down on his bottom lip, returning his stare outside at the world. He couldn't help but think of Delishus and wish she could trade places with Harmony at the moment. But like any other man, King had to play his position and stay home until he saw a good time to leave Harmony's monkey ass behind. He had already heard that she'd been fucking with other niggas while he was gone, but he wasn't going to bring it up because he really didn't care. He was just waiting for the right opportunity to present itself and he would be out. He contemplated his next visit with Delishus, excited that

Harmony would have her friends keeping her busy tomorrow night. His mouth watered for her and he definitely couldn't get her out of his head. Instead of letting her know his plans, he decided to surprise Delishus, feeling that she would be glad to see him, as he was released a few weeks sooner than expected.

King needed a distraction and Delishus was just what he needed. Once again, his everyday drama in life would consist of his baby mama, Harmony and her mother, Debra. Of course he messed around with other females from time to time, but King was torn between Harmony and Delishus. They were like night and day. Harmony had the life most women dreamt of. With the large sum of money that her mother had gotten from her ex-husband who was a preacher, they were doing great financially. Debra's gold-digging ass gave up the church to one of the

deacons and moved on with her life and her late husband's money. For some reason they were blessed; giving them the chance to live the *good* life that most people prayed for.

Being an amateur boxer, King was looking to make it big one day. After meeting Harmony in a club years ago, he found out everything he needed to know about her. He looked forward to Harmony's investments in his dream of becoming a legend in the ring. Unfortunately for King, he couldn't leave the streets alone. He'd been in and out of the prison system since he was a teenager. King couldn't focus on his future because he was too busy destroying the present with his past antics.

Harmony never gave him any doubt about loving him, but over the past few years, she became conceited and spent most of her money partying. For the first year, he tried being faithful to Harmony, but once she refused to give up her life of drugs and partying, he decided to live his life just as she was. King only had a high school education and Harmony always pushed him to go to college, which he didn't want to do.

Damn it feels good to be a free man again! King thought to himself. He just hoped he could stay out of jail long enough to enjoy life with Delishus. Who knows, maybe she could be the woman he needed to keep him out of the streets. King wasn't counting on it though; the streets seemed like a sinkhole, as it always sprung up out of nowhere sucking him back in. He wanted this time to be different, but only time would tell.

CHAPTER 2: WELCOME HOME
KING

People screamed "Surprise" the moment King walked into his house. The hood always showed appreciation when one of their comrades returned from doing time. King had only been gone for almost a year, but it seemed like he had been gone for a while. The time before he did a whole year behind bars so they were even happier about the shorter sentence. There was a "Welcome Home" sign and cake, along with barbecued ribs, chicken, fried fish, steaks, and a variety of other down south foods. Most of his family pitched in to make sure there was enough food for a block party, in case others from the neighborhood decided to come. Everyone greeted King with hugs and kisses showing their love, including his son, Kaden, and daughter, Kamil, who were only a year apart. He walked off with his kids and talked with them for a little while. King didn't really have a close relationship with them, but he really wanted to be a better father. Still, with all the drama his baby mama brought to the table, he had his mind on something else.

"Hey baby boy!" his uncle Bo said the moment he entered the kitchen. They had a card game of *Spades* going at the dining room table. Loud marijuana was in the air, long blunts were being passed around and alcohol was in abundance at his leisure. His uncle got up to hug and pat him on the back. Bo was damn near like his father: tall, dark and in his early fifties, with two open-faced golds in his mouth.

"Hey old man!" King said with a smile. Bo took a few playful swings, as King dodged them and threw out a couple playful haymakers in his direction. King was a full-time dope boy and part time boxer before he went to prison. His dreams of becoming a boxer were put on hold when he met Harmony and got her pregnant. He wasn't getting his weight up to his liking in the ring and, by the time he got his money up to venture into boxing tournaments, he found himself tied up in the justice system. His uncle always tried to get him out of the streets, and took on the role of being his personal trainer in hopes of keeping him alive.

"Alright, now that you're back we have to get to the gym Monday. I don't want you partying and eating too much over the weekend! We have conditioning Monday through Wednesday and come Friday I want you to get on the scale so we can see what class we will be working towards. Glad you kept working out while you were away," Bo said. He held his face and looked him in his eyes. "You got you some pussy yet?" said he asked, smiling.

"What kind of question is that?" King asked.

Then Harmony butted in. "My man ain't getting in no ring so he can get his ass knocked out! He needs all his teeth. I don't want no man with black eyes walking through the malls with me. They may think he's a sissy or something!"

"Well if you had faith in yo' man like we did, then that would be the least of your concerns," King's best friend, Maliki, interrupted.

"Nigga, I have faith in King but, like I said, we need him around here for *other* things. If he can't make any money to feed his family, then he's wasting his time!" she said, rolling her eyes.

"A life in the *ring* is a lot healthier than a life in the *streets!*" Bo said, shaking his finger at Harmony. They were arguing as if King wasn't even in the same room. He knew how bitter Harmony was about his dreams of boxing. It took one amateur fight of him getting knocked out for her to say he needed to quit.

"Harmony, we are running out of room on the table. Where you want us to put this stuff?" one of King's cousins asked.

"Um, I guess I will have to see if we have another table that I can bring out. Here I come," she replied, sharing a quick glance at each of the men before walking out of the kitchen.

"Damn, why are you still with her crazy ass anyway?" Maliki asked, walking up and hugging King. Harmony wasn't everyone's favorite person and she damn sure didn't like anyone who influenced King to continue his boxing career. She loved the fact that he ran the streets moving pills, pounds of Kush and cooking up his own cocaine. She was infatuated with hood niggas, trap Kings and so fourth.

"Man, don't start that shit. You know that's my baby. She's just looking out for me, that's all," King said in defense. But he had a devious smile on his lips.

"Any woman that doesn't mind her man making illegal money, knowing he is risking his freedom, is not a woman looking out for her man. I'ma find you a good Christian woman and see how you like that! These thots these days transform after you really get to know them," Maliki stated. He didn't want to elaborate, but he needed King to comprehend that Harmony wasn't as innocent as she seemed.

"Chill man, come on. Let's not do this today. I'm just getting home and I want today to go smooth, without any bullshit going on, aight?" King said, giving a brotherly handshake to Maliki. Their eyes fixed on one another, King and Maliki had a good solid bond, they had secrets of crimes that they had committed together and to this day, and they'd kept it official.

"Aight, but just for you," he said, taking his seat back at the table and picking up his cards. He placed his lit cigar back into the crevice of his mouth. Smoke curled around his face.

"I wish y'all would sit down and get this ass whoopin'!" King's neighbor, Chaz, teased them, laughing while he counted the possible wins in his hand. They all laughed while King pulled up a chair. He sat next to his cousin Tori, who favored his father, Bo, identically in features. King wasn't bothered that he didn't speak to him.

Even though they were family, Tori always had a hint of jealousy for King and wanted to be in his shoes. He often joked about King not being the man he used to be, claiming that he was running into the ring, because he was scared of the streets. And on the same token, Tori was smooth, handsome and had a strong street reputation, he was knee deep in the drug game and had a couple of bricks of cocaine stashed away. He was doing numbers and doing good for himself. And that alone had him feeling himself and gave him a cocky attitude.

"Tori, why didn't you speak to your cousin man? Aren't you glad to see him out?" Maliki asked, taking a look at his cards to figure out his next move. Tori finally glanced up from his hands full of cards. He had a scar under his eye from when he and King got into a fistfight about a year ago. The cut he'd suffered when King busted his eye open hadn't really healed properly. Tori's hair was dreaded and plaited into one long braid. He had so many tattoos that no one could read them individually unless they were up close.

"Shit, that nigga done been in prison before. What's the big deal about him getting out today? Y'all didn't have me no party when I came home from YDC that time," Tori responded bitterly. He and King were first cousins, but he was tired of his father treating King more like a son than a nephew. Tori was older and he taught King everything he knew, but nobody remembered that. Everyone treated King like he was that nigga, but Tori refused to kiss his little cousin's ass.

"Sounds like something a hater would say," Maliki interjected.

"YDC? Really? Man, that was over ten years ago! Back then every one of y'all bad asses was all in and out of the juvenile system. Who the hell had money to throw parties every week for y'all like that?" Uncle Bo said laughing.

"Naw, it's cool Unc, he ain't got to say a damn thing to me," King said, making direct eye contact with Tori to let him know he would fuck him up if he said the wrong words right now. King didn't spare anyone when it came to respecting him. If they disrespected him or someone he cared about, he would make sure they felt the pain. He and Tori used to hang tight until he started acting shady towards him.

"Aight then, let's keep playin' then. Whose turn is it?" Tori said, changing the subject.

"Here you go baby," Harmony said, walking back into the kitchen to hand him a plate of food. She brought him a canned Sprite and a double shot of Vodka, which was his usual alcoholic pleasure. Maliki cut his eyes at Tori, following them as they connected with Harmony's. She broke her stare first and looked back at King.

"Thank you boo," King responded. Tori sucked his teeth and played with a plastic straw he had sticking out of his mouth.

"Where my plate at?" Tori asked to no one in particular. But he was trying to be funny.

"Nigga, get up and go get you something to eat! You ain't got no maids around here," Chaz told him. Harmony giggled and left them in the kitchen to continue their card game. But in her mind, she definitely wanted to fix him a plate.

They partied for hours. It wasn't until almost 3 a.m. when everything came to an end. Luckily, all of the kids were gone after midnight, because King and his homies turned the party out, getting real freaky with the women there. He couldn't wait to put everyone out so that he could finally get what he needed from Harmony. Her mother, Debra, was gone to spend the night at a friend's house, so they had the house to themselves.

"Aight man, you know you so wild. Hit me up tomorrow so we can go take care of some business!" King joked with one of his homeboys who decided to ride home with Maliki. They were like brothers and Maliki helped King in the boxing ring from time to time as well. He closed the door and turned around seeing Harmony standing in a pair of black stilettos that matched her black and pink negligee.

"Hell yeah! Ooh wee gurl... Glad I'm home!" He grinned as her breasts spilled over the top of the bra. "I like that... Did I ever tell you how much I love you?" King said with an intoxicated slur. He always had to be drunk to have sex with Harmony. That helped to ease the discomfort since he really didn't want to be there.

She motioned for him to come to her before saying, "Come get your pussy, baby. I've been waiting for this for soooo long... I need to feel you... I want you to fuck me like you never have before."

"You don't have to tell me twice! Bring yo' sexy ass over here," he said, staggering in her direction. She hated when King got sloppy drunk because it often kept him from performing the way she was used to. He followed her to the bedroom, making sure he gripped her waistline. He smacked her on the ass, making it clap. Her round ass was the only thing that made up for her ugly face. King bit down on his lip, anticipating the moment where he could dive into her wetness. Harmony turned around and began to removing his shirt, exposing his massive chest and broad shoulders. After sucking on his neck, she kissed his chest and rubbed his muscles, knowing the best way to turn him on.

"Let momma take care of you. Take those pants off and lay down," she whispered. King didn't waste any time. He fumbled with his pants until he finally got the button and zipper undone. He dropped his boxer briefs and remained naked with only his socks on. She turned on her favorite song, "Straight Fucking" by Tyrese. She moved her body, dancing exotically for him, while making her own ass cheeks slap together. The gyrating alone, made King lose his mind. She put on a good show, popping on her knees before slowly prancing over to the bed. Once Harmony saw that he was comfortable on the bed, she climbed on top of him, taking her position on his face. King slid her thong to the side while spreading her plump lips on her vagina as they stared back at him. It had been a while since he ate some pussy, so he took his time tasting her juices. In his mind, her pussy tasted just like Jiffy cornbread. Harmony rode his tongue like she was on a horse. She reached back, stroking his manhood and preparing it for what was to come. He moaned and lapped her sweet nectar, feeling as if he was about to explode. She spread her legs wider, planting her feet steady, as she knew he was about to make her river flow.

Sex with Harmony was always the best. It's the main reason why King kept her around. No one put it down like her in the bedroom and the energy between them always matched. But for some reason, tonight his motivation came from Delishus. Just the thought of her pictures from earlier made him imagine that he was actually giving her oral pleasure instead of Harmony. Maybe that's the Jiffy cornbread taste that was in his mind, soft, sweet and Delishus.

"Ooohhh that feels goooood..." Harmony moaned. Her hormones were so out of control that it took only a couple minutes for her to feel a burst of ecstasy. King was so into the moment that she had to place her hand on his head to make him stop giving her oral pleasure. She climbed out of the bed and summoned him to come to her. Once she got on her knees, he knew what time it was.

"I want you to cum in my mouth, daddy," Harmony told him, bringing him to the edge of the bed. She returned to stroking his dick before she devoured it. She slobbered and bobbed her head, giving him everything he needed. Her head game was on point but after ten minutes, her knees were beginning to hurt. To help him catch a quick nut, she tongued his balls and sucked on them as if they were her favorite fruit. Nevertheless, she returned to deep throating him, giving King the right pleasure to bring him to his peak. Once she sucked him dry, he shivered and fell back onto the bed.

While still fully erect, she turned around and sat on his lap. King loved for her to ride him, but never expected her to ride him like this. She grinded her hips, aggressively bouncing up and down. The heels helped her dance and twerk on his stick as if she was aiming to win a fuck contest. She grabbed his ankles tight, making sure he hit her g-spot just how she wanted him to. Unable to control himself, he thrust back harder and harder until he felt himself explode inside of her swollen walls. She reached orgasm seconds later, giving him a break. They climbed into the bed and drifted off to sleep. If Harmony knew Delishus was still on King's mind, she would have seen the drama heading her way. But as usual, Harmony was blinded by love and thought that she was the only woman who would ever hold King's heart. King drifted off to sleep as his first meeting with Delishus invaded his dreams.

******

"I know you did not just scratch my door with that cart!" Delishus shouted at an older white woman.

"It's not my fault! You parked close to my car and I couldn't get by!" the woman argued.

"Well you need to give me your insurance information. You should have it considering how you've been driving since the Stone Ages! I'm not paying a dime to repair it! Look at my door!" Delishus yelled, getting in the woman's face. Funny how a minor scratch made her erupt with anger.

She had on a pink wrap dress that hugged her voluptuous curves perfectly. Her makeup was flawless and her hair was pinned up in a gorgeous bun. King was parked next to them and couldn't help but overhear the conversation. He walked around and was blown away by her beauty and curvaceous frame. He had never been attracted to plus-sized women, especially not in the city of Atlanta for what they had to offer, but the minute he locked eyes with Delishus he wanted her. Her caramel skin and pretty hazel eyes had him weak in the knees. He didn't understand why such a pretty woman, had such a nasty attitude.

"How would you like it if I pushed my cart into your car?" Delishus asked the woman. She nearly ran her cart *full of groceries into the woman's car, until King grabbed the cart and tried to bring peace to what was on the verge of becoming a disturbing scene.*

"Don't you dare hit my car or I'll call the police! SECURITY!" the woman started calling out.

"Hey, hey, hey...there's no need for of all this. Let me take care of the damages for you, sweetheart. She's an old woman and it's clear that she hit your truck on accident," he said to Delishus. He pulled out a wad of cash. "Miss Lady, my friend here doesn't mean to be rude, but you could at least apologize for scraping her paint. The parking spaces are close, so it isn't her fault she had to park her truck like this. Can we call it a truce? No need to involve security," King said politely to the woman. She mean-mugged Delishus and cut her eyes at her before speaking.

"I guess so... I am sorry if I messed up your paint. I can give you my insurance information, but it will ruin my

rates," the woman stated. She actually started sounding a little sad.

"That won't be necessary, I—" King started to say until Delishus cut off his words.

"The hell it ain't necessary! I don't care about her rates going up! I got the Allstate man on my side, and if I put in a claim, my insurance will want to know who was responsible. Why should I take the blame for this when one of the Golden Girls is at fault?" she ranted.

"Wait a minute, calm down… Like I was saying, I will take care of the scratch, but please be more careful when pushing these carts around, because I'm sure if the shoe was on the other foot you would want this nice young lady to help repair the scratch she put on your car," King said to the woman while standing in front of Delishus.

"I guess you're right. Thank you, young man. Here, it's only a fifty, but it should help fix the paint," the woman said, putting the cash in King's hand and walking away.

She got in her car and drove off, leaving Delishus confused and King feeling like he was the man.

"What the hell am I going to do with fifty? Un uh, bring yo'ass back over here, we are not done talking! I want—"

"What's your name, beautiful?" King asked, stepping in front of Delishus again, cutting off her approach.

"It's about to be 'Whoop A Nigga Ass' in a few seconds!" she angrily stated.

"A pretty thang like you shouldn't act that way in public sweetie. Yeah, she only gave you a few dollars, but that's the part where you come out on top. I said let me take care of the damages, so why are you still angry?" King asked. He counted out a couple hundred-dollar bills and handed them to her along with the fifty.

Delishus accepted the money, feeling a little embarrassed about her behavior. She finally decided to soften up, but kept up her guard because she didn't know what his real intentions were. "Why do you keep saying nice things about me?" she asked.

"I'm just being honest with you, baby, that's the type of man that I am. Guess you ain't used to having a man tell you how pretty you are. What's wrong with me telling you the truth? Are you being difficult because you got a man around or something? Please tell me you don't always act like this," King responded, checking his surroundings. Only a few people near the store heard the drama and they were no longer looking in their direction. Still standing on the side of her Avalanche, King stepped in closer, getting a whiff of her perfume. He didn't know the name of it, but it made the monster between his legs come to life.

She giggled at his question. *"Man? No, I don't have a man. I mean I talk to a few brothas, but it's nothing too serious. I can't say that I have a man to call my own, but thanks for the compliment. I'm really not a catty person and I appreciate you stepping up for me. However, you really don't have to pay for the damage. I'll get it fixed* eventually," Delishus said, picking up a couple of bags and attempting to put them in her truck. She dropped a bag containing her soap and personal items. "Shit!" she cursed. "The last thing I need him to know is that I had a yeast infection. I hate that I get one every time I come on my cycle for the month," Delishus mumbled, rushing to pick up her things.

"Let me help you," King offered, opening her truck door. He helped her pick up the fallen merchandise and placed them on the back seat along with some of the bags from her shopping cart.

"Thank you," Delishus said, getting into her truck and starting the engine.

"You're welcome. I kind of feel like you owe me now though," he told her.

"Owe you?" she asked in disbelief. "You can have your money back if that's how you feel."

"No, not like that," King hurriedly answered. "I still never got your name and hopefully that comes with a number too. I would love to take you out some time. Maybe get to know the real you. I'm sure there's more to you than threatening old ladies."

She blushed and nodded her head. "Yeah, that sounds good. My name is Delishus," she flirted, handing him her business card.

"Wow, you model?" he asked. Looking down at the card.

"Yeah, but only part time. I'm hoping to get some full-time work, so I can quit my job at the clinic. I'm a receptionist for now," she answered.

"Cool. This better not be the wrong number either! In fact, I'm calling you right now to make sure… I know how you women do…y'all give a nigga an old card that belong to someone else or either have a new number different from what you gave," King said, pulling out his phone and dialing the number. Her ringtone of Kelis "My Milkshake" began chiming, making her blush with embarrassment even more because she forgot she had it set for that song.

"Milkshake huh?" King teased. His tongue slipped out of his mouth for a second but he made it disappear again.

"Yeah, I love that song. Don't judge me," she laughed, showing off her cute dimples.

"I don't judge nobody, baby, I leave that to the man up above. We're all humans… But I would like to see you again… Don't forget my number… I don't want to call and you say 'who is this?' and then hang up on me," King said as he walked away.

"Okay. No, I won't do that," she told him, bursting into laughter knowing that she had done a couple men like that before. He never imagined he would have feelings for a BBW the way he was for Delishus. Only time would tell how their relationship would blossom.

CHAPTER 3

In school, kids of course teased her for having big breasts and made fun of her for being larger than those in her grade. She would never forget the first time she got into a fight in high school.

"If you don't stand up for yourself, kids will walk all over you Delishus! If anyone hits you, you try to knock their asses out! Stop letting people take your lunch. I notice you come home hungry, and I know how you don't like to miss a meal, let alone a lunch. Use your weight to your advantage. You're bigger and smarter. Those are your two strengths. No one can take that from you. They think you're weak because you show signs of weakness. Bring out that furious side and I bet they don't fuck with you ever again," her grandmother Delores warned.

She never understood what those words meant until she got older. Kids were so cruel. They called her names, resulting in her skipping some classes just to avoid the embarrassment. She lived with her grandmother, so of course she didn't have the best clothes and shoes like some of her peer and that only made things worse. She hated that her parents moved away for their jobs and left her and her brothers behind. She loved her grandmother to death, but knew without a doubt that things would be different had her parents been around. Her grandmother wasn't at all into fashion. As long as their clothes were clean, that was all that mattered to her. She dressed Delishus in thrift store items, making her an instant target for the girls in her age group. One girl in particular was Betty, the head cheerleader of her school. They took most of their classes together and she always seemed to get other kids to tease Delishus. One morning in particular, Betty was in the cafeteria eating as Delishus approached her and sat down right next to her.

"Hey, are you going to drink your chocolate milk?" she asked Betty in the sweetest voice. Not many people were in the cafeteria in the morning, so Delishus often went there before classes started when she was in the ninth grade. For some reason, on this particular day, Betty and a bunch of other students chose to go in for breakfast as well. Delishus was ready to pop off on her and took this as an opportunity to show her just what she was made of. "Ain't no Hoe in my blood" was the statement that was going through her mind at the time.

"No Hungry Hungry Hippo! You can't have my chocolate milk, go get your own! Or why don't you just go get the chocolate milk from your mother. She is a cow right?" Betty said, rolling her eyes. She returned to her conversation with another fellow classmate, thinking her conversation with Delishus was finished. That was a big mistake on her part. Delishus took the milk off of Betty's tray and stood her ground, daring Betty to say something back.

"Hey!" Betty shouted, standing to her feet. The two young ladies had run into each other on other occasions where Betty hit Delishus with a volleyball while in P.E. class. And another time where Betty teased Delishus in class when the teacher called her up to the board to answer questions.

"Bitch, next time I say give me yo' milk or anything else, you better give it to me! Do you understand?" Delishus stated. Today was the day that she planned to *make them fear her since they couldn't respect her. Betty was the perfect person for her to use as an example.*

She'd had enough of the kids pushing her around without her standing up for herself. She had brothers, but she was tired of asking them to fight her battles. She decided that it was time to do that herself. Betty opened her mouth to speak but Delishus opened the milk carton and swallowed the entire carton's content. Shocked at Delishus' bold actions, Betty threw a punch. She stuck Delishus in the gut, which felt like more of a tickle. Delishus chuckled and swung a heavy arm back, handing Betty, sending her flying onto the top of the table. The hit was so intense that her handprint was beginning to show on Betty's face. The whole cafeteria stood up to see what Betty would do next. She always talked a good game and now it was time for her to show what she was really made of. They all looked on in shock as Betty held her face, letting the tears fall before she raced out of the cafeteria. Everyone looked at Delishus in a new light after that. From that day forward, no one else messed with her and she even made a few new friends. One in particular was Toya, who was still her very best friend today.

The sound of beeping horns brought Delishus back to reality. She glanced up into the rear view mirror, spotting a line of cars behind her. The green light ahead sent the Atlanta drivers into a frenzy, as most of them had places to be. She stuck her arm out of the window, giving whoever blew their horn the middle finger.

"Fuck y'all, go around!" she shouted, stepping on the gas pedal. Her appointment at the nail salon was waiting. She needed to get herself pampered and wondered how her day would end.

After going through her call log and seeing missed calls from men she dated a time or two, Delishus threw the phone in her purse and kept it moving. She wasn't interested in any of them, so there was no need to get excited. King had been the only man that she looked forward to seeing. He hadn't responded to her last letter, which made her kind of nervous. He was always quick to reply, so maybe something was wrong. She decided to call her best friend Toya to temporarily help take her mind off of her troubles.

"Hey boo boo, what are you doing?" Delishus asked.

"On my way to Sally's Beauty Supply, you know I have to keep my hair on fleek! How about you, chick?"

"Yeah, I bet. I already know. I'm walking into the nail shop for a spa treatment. We should meet up for drinks later, if you're not too busy. Tell Don he has to let you get out of the house every once in a while," she advised.

"That sounds cool. Don't be hatin' because my man like to be up under me. I will let you know though for real, because I have been craving a Sangria. But on some real shit, have you heard about this guy that tried to kidnap and rape these two women?"

"As much free pussy walking around in Atlanta, I can't imagine a guy trying to rape these thirsty ass women. The news is always exaggerating stories," Delishus responded. She entered the salon and was directed into a chair.

"Well, I'm taking precautions. My precious jewel is not free, and the only way a brother getting some of this is if he pays for it. He can try to take something if he wants to,

I'll cut his dick off and hand it to the police when they come!" Toya laughed. They both giggled.

"The way Don has you locked up in the house, can't no man get to you anyway. What is his name?"

"I don't remember the name, but the news said it's been reported in two urban neighborhoods which mean he likes dark meat," Toya responded.

"Aw shoot, this is Germane calling me again. Let me see what he wants, I'll hit you back in a minute."

"Okay, be careful, and call me when you leave the nail salon," Toya stated.

"Alright...bye," she said, aggravated at Germane's persistent behavior. "Yes," she answered while rolling her eyes.

"Well hello baby, how are you doing?"

"How many times are you going to call me?" Delishus ignored his gentle tone.

"Sorry, did I catch you at a bad time?" he asked from the other end.

"Hell yeah you did and this is your fourth time calling. What is it that you need?" she hollered into the phone.

"Wow! I only wanted to see if you would like to go out for dinner tonight."

"Really? Dinner? You could have texted me that. Look, I apologize if I'm snapping on you. I've never had a man that cared to be around me as much as you. I've had my heart broken so many times that it's hard to see when a man is for real. We went out on a few dates and had sex both times. I don't want you to think that is all it takes to be with me. You seem to have an ulterior motive, but you can keep it moving if you do," she explained. It saddened her that she couldn't spend time with King like she wanted to. And Germane really didn't help by putting pressure on her to be with him. He was nice and well mannered, but he wasn't her King. He'd most definitely claimed his spot in her heart, even after only knowing him for a short period of time.

"My only motive is getting to know you better, but I understand how you feel. I can show you that I can be the man you need me to be and more. Continue with what you were doing and call me whenever you are free."

"Wait, Germane," she said, but he didn't hear her because he disconnected once he said his final peace. Delishus shook him off and popped in her ear buds to listen to music while she got her pedicure. In the back of her mind, she wondered when true love would find her.

******

Delishus scrunched up her toes, examining the red polish that she decided to get. They matched her manicured nails and she was sure they would match the red negligee she had stored in her drawer at home. Her big daddy would be free soon and she knew it would only be a matter of time before he showed up at her door. Delishus was tired of breaking up happy homes and she hated being the side chick. She wanted a man of her own and she refused to settle. None of the men she dated had proposed to her, which was just the way she liked it because she never could see herself with them for a lifetime. Delishus considered herself to be a fuck 'em and leave 'em type of broad. Married men were not her forte. Unfortunately, she ended up finding out that most of the men were married soon after she began having an affair with them. She hoped King was different, but only time would tell.

"No man has power over this pussy!" Delishus would always joke with other women. Deep down inside she felt different about King though.

"Thank you!" she said, walking out of the nail shop.

"Hey pretty lady," an older light-skinned gentleman said, waving at her and flashing his cigarette stained teeth.

"Uh uh Milli Vanilli, I only eat dark chocolate," Delishus Replied, frowning up at the flirting man. He was tall with salt and pepper gray hair. "Plus, you wouldn't know what to do with all this ass if I served it to you in sections!" she told him, pressing the button to unlock her Chevy Avalanche. The man took the hint and laughed, playing off her comment. He just didn't know how serious she was. Delishus was definitely a feisty woman who didn't care about speaking whatever came to her mind. That was exactly the way her grandmother taught her to be.

"Damn it's hot out here!" She complained as the sweat began to form in between her breasts the minute she walked outside. "This is some bullshit! Now I got to get in the tub again!" She added. She always took two baths a day, and hated the feeling of being dirty. As a big girl, she learned how to maintain her sweet scent and fashionable appearance a long time ago.

Once she arrived at her apartment, she noticed a man standing with flowers. Not knowing his intentions, she assumed he was at the wrong door and tried to walk past him. "Um excuse me, but you're blocking my doorway. Can I help you?" she quizzed.

The man turned around, shocked at the beautiful, voluptuous woman that stood before him. He could see exactly why she would be receiving flowers. He looked her up and down, realizing that Delishus was not your average big boned girl. She seemed confident and he could tell that she had a style of her own. Her presence made him nervous, something that had never happened before. He swallowed hard, making sure that he chose his words carefully.

"Sorry, I'm looking for a Delishus Jones," he stated trying to keep his smile friendly.

"Mmm hmm, that's me. But I thought I just told you that you were blocking my doorway. Can I get by, please?" she asked him. Because her apartment rested in the corner of the building, she needed him to step aside in order to get to her door to unlock it.

"Oh, of course," he responded, releasing a slight chuckle.

"If you laugh one more time, I'm gonna think you're being funny instead of charming. I don't know what you're still standing here for. I already said I was the person you are looking for. What else do you need?" she asked, annoyed at his stupid grin. He looked like the Grinch that stole Christmas.

"Well you have to sign for these flowers. Someone ordered to have them delivered anonymously. You must be a very special woman," he said, holding up the box of flowers and the clipboard.

"You damn right I'm special. I do tricks yo' ass couldn't imagine yo' ole lady doin'! Why you think they call me Delishus?" she said, bursting into laughter. Now he was the one, No longer amused with her. "I'm just kidding... Lighten up a little. Stop taking yo' job so serious! All you have to do is bring people mail; you deserve to hear a little humor. Viagra and Molly don't mix," Delishus said, unlocking her door. She kicked it open and tossed her purse onto the couch beside it.

"My wife is deceased so that kind of humor is taken seriously," the deliveryman advised.

"Aw, my bad Morgan Freeman! Well, if you need a curvy woman to lay up with at night, give me a ring. I know how to keep a man satisfied," she said, flicking her tongue at him.

"Please! Just sign the paper ma'am," he interrupted her flirting.

"Nigga, don't be mean! You just said yo' wife dead, so I'm tryna help you out. Give me this damn paper then!" She grabbed the clipboard, scratching his hand in the process.

"Ouch!" he shouted, and then snatched his hand back. "You scratched me!" Delishus ignored him while examining the order sheet, attempting to see who had sent her the flowers. She had been talking to a few dudes lately, so she honestly had no clue that they were from.

"Oh I didn't mean to do that," she said, taking his hand and licking his wound. His scratch wasn't even bleeding, just looked like he was ashy on one part of his hand.

"Ew!" he responded, feeling disgusted with her freakiness. He took the clipboard and hauled ass from her.

"Yeah, you better run before I eat yo' ass for dinner," she said, laughing as he shook his head and rushed back to his delivery van. *I wonder who sent these,* she thought. Delishus opened the box and inhaled the scent of the flowers. Her doorbell rang, catching her off guard. She looked out the peephole but was not able to see because someone obviously placed their finger over it.

"Who is it?" she called out. A few seconds pass without any sound or reply. "Who is it!" she said this time getting an attitude. When she still didn't hear anything, she pulled on the doorknob, cracking it open. The sight before her almost made her heart leap out of her chest. Her knees buckled a little when their eyes met.

"Hey baby," he said in a smooth and easy tone of voice, standing in his blue jean shorts and wife beater. His blue, Air Jordans looked fresh out the box.

"King? When did you get out?" she asked. "Damn, for a jail bird, you sho'll know how to snap back when you're free. Bring yo' sexy ass in here," Delishus said, embracing him in front of her door the moment he entered. He never got a chance to answer her question before she smothered his lips with hers, savoring his juices. She could taste the Winterfresh gum he had previously been chewing on. His cologne, whatever it was, and the tightness of his hug made her want him inside of more than just her apartment. Their tongues played with each other until he finally released her, remembering that they still had the door open.

"I see someone missed me! And once you get to know me better, you'll realize that I always land on my feet no matter what comes my way in life," King informed her, taking a seat on her couch. She closed the door, making her way over to sit next to him.

"Of course I missed you!" she said before slapping him in the chest. She took a seat next to him, ready to devour him.

"What you hit me for woman?" he laughed.

"Because you left me when we were just getting to know each other. I don't want you to ever leave me again, okay?" she demanded. He reached forward, massaging her plump thighs. No other woman filled him up like Delishus.

"I ain't goin' nowhere no time soon. I'm sorry, but you caught me while I was in a rough time, shit was tight. I didn't see that shit coming myself. I do want to thank you for holdin' it down while I was gone though. You didn't give my pussy to anyone, did you?" he asked, making her blush. He slapped her butt as it hung off the edge of the couch.

"Don't play with me, boy! You know this pussy was made for you. Hell no I didn't!" she lied easily, hoping it sounded convincing. Good thing she hadn't had sex since her last encounter with Germane. It had been a couple weeks. She was pretty sure King won't be able to tell. "I know he didn't expect me to wait almost a year for some dick! Is he crazy?" Delishus silently said to herself maintaining an innocent face.

"Why don't we get out of here and go get something to eat. I think I owe you dinner, don't I?" He glanced around, noticing the flowers on the countertop in the kitchen. "Am I interrupting something? Who sent you those?" he asked. He would be lying if he said he wasn't jealous that someone else was pushing up on her while he was locked up. He didn't expect her to be solo until he got out of jail, but he hoped that he hadn't lost his place in her heart. He remembered the first time he met Delishus and was glad that he had in the parking lot.

"I really don't know who sent them. They were just delivered a few moments before you came. There's no sender's name or anything attached."

"Well throw them motherfuckas away! I wanna be the only nigga sending you flowers and shit," he told her, kissing her cheeks and making her smile even harder. Hell, for him she would grind them up in the garbage disposal if he wanted her to. Feeling that she would rather hold on to the flowers a little longer, she grabbed her purse to deflect his attention. They left her apartment to go to a nice restaurant of her choosing. They were too engrossed in their conversation to see Germane sitting in his car a few feet away. He started his engine and drove off, heartbroken that he'd missed a chance to take Delishus out.

The entire time he was out, Harmony buzzed his phone for stupid reasons. She usually didn't call him while she was hanging with her girls. Plus, she said she was going to be home around 1 a.m. so he couldn't understand why she kept calling to try and keep tabs on him.

"Excuse me babe, I gotta run to the restroom real quick," King said, offering an awkward smile. Delishus knew no different from which he spoke so she grinned back and dove into her plate of food.

"Okay baby…don't let anyone steal you while you're on your way there," Delishus joked. She smacked his ass when he went by. It turned him on, but his phone vibration cut his smile short.

"Hello!" King yelled once he got near the restrooms and away from the area their table sat in.

"Nigga! Why the fuck you haven't answered my text? And I called you a few minutes ago too. Where you at?" Harmony said without greeting him with a "hello" back.

"I'm out at the pool hall, over here on the West side with a few niggas. Why you keep calling? I told you this same shit about twenty minutes ago! And I didn't get no text, so how the hell can I respond to something I don't have?" King said, getting pissed off.

"Well I sent you a text with a picture of me asking how I looked. I'll resend it. My bad! Call me when you leave the pool hall. Love you," Harmony replied.

"Uh huh, love you too," he told her hanging up. He didn't care how sweet she tried to sound. He glanced at his phone, realizing that Harmony actually did send him a picture message fifteen minutes ago. He was so into his evening with Delishus that he didn't even pay her message any attention, thinking that it was nothing. He closed the message after responding "SEXY" back to Harmony. King raced back to the table, taking his seat next to her in the booth. He wrapped his arms around her round waist and kissed her neck. Delishus quickly locked the phone once he returned. She had just responded to Germane telling him that she was feeling under the weather and wasn't in the mood for getting out tonight.

"Mmm, what is that smell?" he asked.

"Oh I'm sorry…I wasn't expecting you to come back so soon. My stomach is a little upset; I had to release a little gas," Delishus admitted. King burst into laughter once he realized she didn't comprehend which scent he was referring to.

"What are you talking about? I am talking about the spray or perfume you have on. What's it called?" he said, unable to keep from laughing.

"Aw shit," she said, joining in on his laughter and feeling slightly ashamed for telling him something he really didn't want to know. "It's called 'Glo' by JLo. That's my favorite perfume. I switch up from time to time though. Thanks, do you like it?" she responded.

"Yeah, I love the way it smells on you."

For the next hour and ten minutes, they ate lobster tails, shrimp and fettuccine noodles and Alfredo sauce, with garlic bread. King had had a couple Corona's. They talked and laughed like a couple that had been together for years. When he asked if she ready to leave she nodded while King called for the check. He paid the bill without hesitation. Thankfully, he kept a stash at his uncle's house that Harmony knew nothing about. He wasn't the type of dude to come out of jail without any cash in his pockets. He knew Harmony would have an excuse to spend every dime she could find if she saw it. They left the restaurant and headed for her home. King hoped he would get lucky tonight and have another taste of her sweet honey.

****

They returned to her apartment, kissing and groping on each other. King couldn't stand the fact that he had to go back home to be with Harmony. While he was with Delishus he could relax, be himself. She was infatuated by his ambition to become the 'World's Greatest Boxer'. She was encouraging and believed in him as if she had seen him win a match for herself. Every man needs a strong woman to stand in his corner and, for some reason, he felt that Delishus was that woman so far.

"Next time I take you out, I will make sure it is somewhere less crowded. I got a little jealous seeing how those other men were looking at you. They almost made me get gangsta' up in that place. Fuck around and make me put one of them lames on World Star," King joked.

"Boy whatever! There were hardly any men thinking about me. I saw one or two glance, but it was nothing like how you were seeing them. The only man I saw in there was you," Delishus said sweetly. She was more than confident in her appearance, but sometimes she wondered what attracted such a handsome man like King to her.

"I'm for real. I already know you get a lot of compliments, so don't front. But you made a nigga feel lucky tonight, I swear," King told her, leaning in to kiss her again. Instead of leaving, he lifted her shirt over her head and began planting kisses on her neck and chest. Her breathing got heavy, making her breasts rise and fall the more he turned her on. She fondled his body, feeling on his chest underneath his shirt. Her fingers traced his muscles and tattoos.

"I want you, King and I really like you. Don't play with my heart though, because I'm a fatal attraction type of bitch. I'll fuck your life up if you bring games to my house," she warned, interrupting the mood. He placed a finger to her lips, hushing her, and then went back to massaging her breasts. They moved into the bedroom where he could enjoy every inch of her body. She shivered at his touch. The moment he pulled down her skirt, she hid herself.

"What are you doing?" he asked. He removed her hands as they covered up her stomach. It was more of a shield from him seeing her panties.

"I don't want you seeing me like this. Can we please turn off the lights?" she asked.

"No woman, are you serious? I want to see you. Last few times we had the lights off and I could barely find you in the room," he teased. She offered a smirk and laughed. King tugged at her red panties, tossing them to the side. King spread her thighs, pressing her up against the wall. Taking his fingers, he gently spread the doors of her wet box and sucked on her clit until she began gripping his head and forcing his tongue to dig deeper into her slit. Her vagina throbbed and soaked on his tongue, bringing her to an unexpected orgasm that caused her to scream blissfully after a few minutes. King had his hands full, but he wanted to show her how much he'd appreciated her. He made his tongue slide in and out of her pussy until it spit up, her cum juices tasted so good. The way she was shivering and shaking, he knew she was enjoying every bit of it. He looked up at her.

"You okay, baby?" he asked, noticing her biting down on her lip. He could feel her knees buckle and confirmed his job was done. He guided her over to the bed and let his shorts fall to the floor. He smiled when he saw her shocked expression. Guess she forgot how thick and long he really was. King had the physique of a body builder and every muscle he had bulged when he got completely naked, including the muscle between his legs. He laid her on the bed, squeezing her thighs and legs. His erection seemed to aim straight in her direction as if it knew exactly where its home was.

Once he grabbed her feet, he massaged them and placed them on his hard erection. Delishus went wild when he forced her legs open and shoved his nine inches inside of her wetness. *This what got me fucked up now. A thick woman, close built, and a tight ass grippin' pussy.* He thought to himself. Playtime was over and King didn't hold back. He pumped hard and fast at first, making their bodies begin to sweat. Then he slowed his movement down, making her feel every inch of his dick. Ten minutes turned to thirty and now the smell of nothing but good fucking was in the air. King was going side to side and hitting every corner, making sure his dick touched every sensitive spot she had. She couldn't help it, she was coming all over him, and the sheets were soaked now. Holding one of her legs on his shoulder, he found the leverage that he needed, allowing him to hit corners on her vaginal walls that she never knew existed. Delishus moaned and shook her head as if an exorcism were being performed on her. She began to soak the sheets the more he plunged inside of her, pulling out and driving himself back in deeper. Once he felt himself beginning to cum, he pulled up her other leg wrapping them around his neck. The faster he stroked, the more he came. Forgetting that he didn't wear a condom, he prayed that Delishus was on some kind of birth control. His first thought, of course, was to make sure that he pulled himself out just in time to release his semen. But the minute he started to bust, he couldn't stop. The feeling of being inside of her hot juiciness took over his mind. It was the best sex he'd had in a long time compared to his night with Harmony. King dropped her legs and fell onto the bed beside her. They both attempted to control their breathing but knew it would take a few moments before they could.

"Wow..." Her mouth formed a perfect 'O'. "That was amazing," Delishus cooed. King checked his phone realizing that it was almost 2 a.m. and they'd been making love for hours.

"Shit!" he cursed in a panic. Harmony had already called him more than ten times. "I gotta go baby," he told her.

"Huh? Where are you goin'?" Delishus asked in confusion. She sat up on the bed, pulling the sheets up to cover her breasts. She watched him gather his things and his actions reminded her of the other men she had brought home. Once they got what they wanted, they didn't hesitate to leave her.

"I have to get home," he told her, putting on his shoes. She laughed with disappointment.

"Mmm hmm, I can't believe I thought you were actually different. Go on then. Get out!" she told him, jumping up from the bed. If he wanted to leave, then she may as well help him to the door. Delishus grabbed a nighty from her drawer and quickly put it on. She pushed King as he was tying up his shoes, making him fall onto the floor.

"What da' fuck you trippin' fa'?" he asked upset.

"Because you came into my house today *acting* like you wanted to be with me. You feed me good food, and damn good dick only to disappear when I need you around the most. I don't want just sex King. I can get that from anywhere. If you can't handle being in a relationship, then I want you out of my house and out of my life. Don't come back until you can be the man that I need you to be!" she fussed. He stood up, attempting to plead his case.

Delishus opened the door, ignoring him. "Delishus, please hear me out. I'll explain everything to you when the time is right." She slammed the door in his face the moment he was outside. He knew he didn't have time to deal with her while Harmony was calling him, so he ran to his car and headed home. Nights like this made King wish he was a single man. The women in his life seemed to bring him nothing but problems.

Smashing on the gas, King zipped through her apartment parking lot before jumping onto the street. He ran a red light going at the speed of what he thought could get him successfully through it. The couple of beers he had at the restaurant had him so tipsy that he didn't realize his mistake until it was too late. He didn't see it, but another vehicle came out of nowhere and slammed right into him. The loud crunching sound of metal made King's eardrums pop. His neck and head snapped forward so hard that he swore he heard something crack. Glass shattered from all directions and he could feel himself throwing up in the car after becoming dizzy from the whirlwind he was caught in. No doubt, his collision with another vehicle halted traffic, resulting in honking horns and tires screeching against the asphalt street. King's body jerked hard to the left, once the Chevy Malibu he was driving stopped spinning. If he had worn a seat belt, he wouldn't have gone flying out of the window. He felt his body soaring into the air until it crashed hard into the pavement. Out of the corner of King's eye, he saw other cars coming, as well as people rushing to see about his condition. He heard voices of concern, but after a few seconds, everything went black.

CHAPTER 4

Harmony needed to make sure that King wasn't on his way home. After calling and texting, she didn't get a response. She knew his ass was out doing something that he had no business doing. "I'm glad he went out with his niggas tonight, tuh. At least I have about another couple hours before he expects me to be home," she said to herself. She drove fast to see her side nigga, knowing their secret love affair required her to make unsuspected visits when possible. She got out of the car, tripping over her heel and nearly breaking it.

"What are you doing drinking?" he asked once she staggered up to his door.

"Don't tell me what to do! You ain't my man, yet," she replied, brushing him off. Tori frowned at her, shaking his head at the same time and wondering why she decided to come over during this time of night.

"Where you been at?" Tori asked.

"I was out with Tiffany and Savannah. Those two girls are so crazy. We had a blast down at the club. But after we left, I wanted to see my boo thang so I decided to come over here," she responded, taking a seat on his couch. Her legs were so gapped open that he could see her cooch. Harmony hardly wore any panties at times. She definitely didn't wear any when she wore a dress that, in her opinion, was made for wearing without panties. Tori closed the door, locked it, and then walked over to the leather loveseat where she was and sat next to her. "I missed you. And you never did answer my question the other day. How long are you goin' to keep on playin' my cousin? We might as well go ahead and let it be known that I'm yo' nigga now," Tori said as he got comfortable and spreading her thighs while rubbing on them.

"See, let me stop you right there. I ain't playin' nobody, I'm just trying not to get played. King is the one who loves me, while you up here tryna trap me. You could have pulled out and jacked off or something to get a nut, but nawl, what you do? Now you got me pregnant and shit, and you knew I was with him to begin with. I feel like you played me," she advised, poking him in the arm.

"I didn't play you baby. I fucks with you the long way, I really was just keepin' his pussy in order for him while he was gone." Tori said, taking his hand and massaging her breasts. Her nipples were growing hard under his touch.

"Well now you can fuck wit' this baby the long way too. But chill out with all that hatin' on my nigga, King. He was here before you, so he always gonna be at the top."

"So you just want me to be your fun nigga, yo entertainment nigga on the side?" Then he frowned a little and thought about what she said and added. "And I don't hate on nan' nigga, let's get that straight." Tori said while placing his hand on her stomach.

"Fun nigga, side nigga, or whatever you wanna call it. Can you prove that you deserve his spot? What can you do for me that King can't?"

"I can do a whole lot more than he can! Give me the chance to show you," he told her while kissing on her earlobe. Sliding his hand between her legs, he moved a couple fingers inside of her vagina, finding her already wet and eager to be with him. She giggled at his actions, knowing exactly where the conversation was leading to. She gave him a smile, then let out a small moan and grabbed his dick through his jeans.

"You say that now, but King doesn't know this is your baby. I need to keep it that way until this shit passes over," she told him, bracing herself for his reaction.

"Huh? Why? Hell nah! This is my seed and I'm claiming it. King already has everything and I'll be damned if he gets the pleasure of having my son calling him daddy and shit," Tori said with a slight tone of aggression in his voice.

"But it won't get that far. Trust me. I got everything working the way I need it to right now. Don't mess things up for our future. If you want to be with me, then you will have to let me do what is necessary," Harmony said, grabbing him by his shoulders. She drew him near and kissed him. He could smell the alcohol on her breath.

"Alright, I guess. I trust you baby, but sooner or later we gonna have to get shawty out the way," he said, then added, "Now come on give daddy some of that wet wet," Tori responded, placing his hand behind her head. He guided her down on her knees. *This bitch ain't about to fuck with my head, unless it's the head on my dick! I bet I have the final say so when it comes to my kid!* Tori silently said to himself.

Harmony unzipped his pants and followed his unspoken orders. She reached in, finding his hard erection and brought it to her mouth. Tori was hooked the first time she gave him some head; her thick lips were soft and wet. He, on the other hand, was the opposite of King, in that he actually had true feelings for Harmony. Shit, to him she was the prettiest and realist woman in the world. Money wasn't something he needed since he hustled in the streets getting his own. He figured that having a down ass bitch like Harmony on his side would put him on the map.

With her by his side, he wanted to take over the streets and do things bigger and better than King ever did. Funny how a woman could cloud the judgment of a man so quickly. Tori placed his hand behind her head and enjoyed her warm mouth. She may be trash to King, but Tori considered her to be his Queen. And in his head, he would do anything to be with her.

CHAPTER 5

After creeping in the house and finding King still not there, she laid down in bed and tried to gather her thoughts between King and Tori. Her phone rang and the call that she received sent her into panic mode. Harmony rushed out of the house and headed straight to Grady Memorial Hospital.

The following day, they'd realized that King wasn't hurt as bad as it looked. Harmony wheeled him out of the hospital, fussing the entire way home. He didn't even get a chance to clear his head before she started talking to him as if he were her child, instead of her boyfriend. He could remember leaving Delishus' house last night and thanked God that he didn't end up in worse condition than he was in. A couple bruises and cuts resulted from the car crash that he was involved in less than twenty-four hours ago. Being that he was ejected from the car, that was nothing compared to how bad it could have been.

That's what I get for being some place I had no business being. Pussy done damn near got me killed. I should have just stayed over Delishus' house and made up an excuse for Harmony, he thought to himself, slowly shaking his head side to side.

"I don't know why you always doin' stupid shit! You messed up my damn Hybrid!" Harmony fussed, interrupting his marinating thoughts.

"Fuck that raggedy ass car! You should be worried about me!" King shouted at her with a twisted and angry look on his face. The nerve of this bitch.

"I'm worried about you messing up my damn credit by totaling out a car with *my* name on it! You can't even afford to pay for it to get fixed!"

"I'll get that bullshit repaired, I promise," King replied, holding his head as it continued to throb.

"You better believe you gonna fix it nigga! Broke ass stay fuckin' up! That's why you need to be in school! We could have been getting a school check and you could be in a lab or even better the trap making some real dough," she continued ranting while hitting the steering wheel with the palm of her hand. Harmony advised King that he should go to school for Chemistry, after suggesting that they sell crystal meth to increase their income. Methamphetamine was becoming one of the most profitable drugs in the city and climbing in their neighborhood.

"Well if that's all you care about, we don't need to be together then! A degree doesn't make me a man. I ain't the type of dude to sit in no lab all day, sweating over some explosive shit! I want to fight! I'm good at knocking motherfuckers out! Keep on running yo' mouth and you gonna be able to attest to that for real!" he threatened.

Whenever he talked of leaving Harmony, she would change her attitude quick. She could take dissing and down-talking him, but if he ever mentioned breaking up with her, she instantly started apologizing. Harmony yanked on the steering wheel, making a hard left. Her driving was worse than his on any day that he drove sober.

"Boy, you ain't goin' nowhere. You know I care about you. Stop acting all weak and shit," softening her voice a little.

"I'm not actin' like nothing! I damn near died and here you go coming at me about a car when that can easily be replaced. What if I died? There's only one original King Brice around this bitch! You didn't say you were glad I'm alive or even act happy that I wasn't hurt more seriously!" King said in anger. He brought his own headache to a higher level of pain.

Harmony slammed on the brakes after noticing that she was approaching a red light. "You better stop raising your voice at me. I said I was sorry bookie-wookie. I love you, okay? I rushed over here as soon as I got the call. It's just that you know we been dipping in that money and if we get too low then I will need to get a job, unless you want your bitch to start selling Mollies again. Now come on, be a little more responsible next time, boo," she suggested in a more concerned tone now. He remained quiet, pressing his lips together.

"Do you forgive me?" she asked, placing her hand on his thigh.

"I guess," King mumbled right as they pulled up to the house.

"Very well then." As she was parking, she looked around and saw a woman standing nearly at the edge of their driveway. "Wait, is that the Delishus chick I saw on your phone? What the fuck is she doing outside of my house? Oh I forgot, that's family right?" Harmony said sarcastically once they rolled up to their crib. You would think with all the money her mother, Debra received that she would have bought them a mini mansion in Buckhead somewhere, but instead, she decided to buy a two-story house on the outskirts of the hood in College Park, like she was average. A white, four-bedroom house contained a huge yard, with a pool in the back. The community wasn't even gated but, with King being in the house, they didn't have to worry about any break-ins, or anyone stealing their cars.

Harmony gave King an evil stare before turning quickly into the driveway. The coupe came to a stop so hard that when she put the gear in park, King's head tilted forward unexpectedly striking a pain in his neck.

"Damn Harmony, you gonna put me back in the hospital driving like a fuckin' maniac!" He fussed at her while rushing to get out of the car first. Having Delishus pop up at his house was sure to bring drama. He didn't even know how she knew where he lived.

"Yo' cousin, huh? I want to hear this conversation. Go ahead and see what the bitch wants," Harmony said, following him towards the side of the street.

"Oh my god King, are you okay?" Delishus said, palming his face once he was near her.

"Hey Delishus, this isn't a good time right now. You can't be here. How did you find out where I lived?" he asked. *This bitch is on some P.I. shit!* King thought.

"Why the hell is she caressing yo' face? What type of incest shit y'all country assess got goin' on?" Harmony said, following their every move.

"Well when you crashed into that car, I ran up to see if you were still alive. I saw your address on your driver's license. I called for an ambulance and gave them your I.D. I decided to wait until you got released from the hospital to come and see you," Delishus advised, reaching out to hug him. King dodged her, deflecting her touch this time, knowing that Harmony was within earshot.

"Hey, I'm Harmony, King's fiancé," she finally snapped with a, attitude. "You're his cousin, right?" Harmony asked, cocking her head to the side while trying to get a glimpse of King's facial expression. If she could see the worried look on his face, he'd be caught dead in his ways. But everything that happens in the dark comes to light, so whether she could see his face or not, King was heading straight into a dead end with his lies.

"Uh excuse me? Cousin. No, I'm—"

"Alright thank you for coming to check on me. But I got to handle some business, so holla at me later. As a matter of fact, I'll just call you if I need anything." King said, walking Delishus to her truck to stop her from finishing her sentence.

"Something isn't right here. Why did she just call me your cousin? And is she really your fiancée?" Delishus quizzed. He continued to usher her into her truck, but Delishus turned around to give Harmony her full attention. Since he wanted to play games, she decided to show him that she didn't take kindly to lying dogs.

"Don't try to whisk her away now! I know one damn thing, if she ain't yo' cousin, I'm about to ruffle some feathers off this bird, cuz ain't no bitch you creepin' with gon' show up to my motha' fuckin' house like I ain't shit!" Harmony said loud enough for the entire neighborhood to hear.

"Like I said, I am not his cousin, King is my man! And he didn't tell me about being engaged. Judging by what he has at home, I can tell why he's out roaming the streets looking for a real bitch to keep him warm at night!" Delishus said, walking towards Harmony. They were only a couple feet away from each other. King was desperate to keep the two women from attacking one another. He jumped in front of Delishus, grabbing her arms, forcing her back to her truck for the second time.

"What the fuck I just say Delishus? Take yo' ass home!" he shouted. She stared at him in shock. He'd never raised his voice at her or even sounded harmful. This wasn't the man she met months ago. Tears came out of nowhere, but she slowly turned until Harmony opened her big mouth to say something smart.

"The fuck is she talm' bout'? Yo, you betta get her ass away from here! I'm already on probation because of that other fat ass bitch, Talia, you had me fighting over you! Every time I turn around it's a different bitch coming to my house! Yo' ass is about to be homeless!" Harmony warned, pointing at him. Delishus had been sitting on the hood of her car waiting for him to get home, not knowing that he lived with another woman. Her heart was broken and hate for him flooded her thoughts. It was obvious from now on that the two women would forever hate each other because they both loved King.

"Harmony, go in the house!" King demanded. He turned and faced Delishus and began whispering to her. "Look, this is my baby mama. We got two kids together and she wants me to marry her. I want you though and I'm planning on leaving her soon. But I need a little more time, okay? Go home and I promise I will call you later tonight."

"I'll leave if that's what you want King, "she said in a low tone of voice and went on. "But you definitely got some explaining to do for real. I only came over because I felt bad for letting you drive. I shouldn't have let you do that, considering you had those beers at the restaurant. I'm so sorry," she said, embracing him for a hug. Caught off guard, King held his hands out showing Harmony his innocence. Delishus squeezed his body up to hers, holding onto him tight and making Harmony jealous on purpose.

"Aw hell naw!" he heard Harmony shout. The heels on her stilettos clicked faster and faster as she raced over to attack them.

"Aaaggghhhh!" King yelled, trying to release Delishus' grip on him. The two women battled for King, pulling him left and right until Harmony felt she wanted to take her anger further. She grabbed a hand full of Delishus' hair and swung mighty blows wherever she was able to land them. The two women screamed and cursed, turning a calm situation into something portrayed on WWE Raw. King's heart seemed to be the prize up for grabs. Harmony was taller than Delishus, weighing in right over a hundred pounds. King was looking around and hoping that no one was recording the fight on their phone.

"Stop that! Ay, let go of her hair!" King hollered. His words didn't reach the ears of either woman, because Delishus finally broke free and pushed Harmony with all her might. The embarrassing fall Harmony sustained sent her into a bigger frenzy.

"I said break it up!" King said, finally getting a chance to come between the women.

"She started it with her Rupal-looking ass!" Delishus said, swinging and missing Harmony.

"Bitch please, he don't want yo' sloppy ass!" Harmony shouted back. Her chest heaved as she tried to catch her breath.

"Whatever, you wish you had all this ass I got! I'm a Glamazon! You're the one standing ova there looking anorexic. You hungry…huh? Is that why you're so upset? You need me to buy you something to eat?" Delishus taunted.

"Fuck a Glamazon, bitch you look like you were raised in the damn Amazon. Big ass slut! Big Foot lookin' ass BITCH. I got money!" Harmony said, taking a couple bills from her purse and tossing them into Delishus' face.

She picked up a couple bills, throwing them in King's face. "I don't need your money! This joker here must need it though. As a matter of fact, that has to be all he cares about to be living with you! Loose pussy ass bitch. He doesn't really want to be with you either! Not when he can have all of this!" Delishus said, smacking her ass and taunting Harmony more. King put his hand to her mouth, shushing Delishus, trying to kill the chaotic vibe.

"Whatever, get off my property! I'm calling to report you for trespassing!" Harmony warned, straightening up her curls that seemed to be tangled after Delishus caught her fingers in them. She pulled King in the direction of the house in which he didn't refuse. Delishus was left standing in the yard, removing her synthetic wig. She was sweaty and pissed off for even being put in this predicament.

"It's a free country; I can go anywhere I want! He may be goin' in the house with you now, but he was with *me* last night!" Delishus shouted, making Harmony stop in her tracks.

"What's she talking 'bout King?" Harmony asked forcing King's hand from hers. He shook his head at Delishus urging her not to spill the beans on their secret affair.

"Nothing. I don't know what she talkin' bout babe, I swear. Delishus go on with that bullshit! You makin' my spot hot and I've told you before that me and you are over wit!" King said. It was him who was now pulling Harmony towards the house, trying to get her inside.

"Forget you King! She deserves to know what kind of dog ass nigga you are. Yeah, he was at my place last night! And we had sex! That eggplant he got down there ain't yours by yourself no more. That's why he was in a car accident near my place. Open your eyes and wake up. Better yet, never mind. I forgot, it's too hard for you to get another man. Hang on to him all you want, but I'm done. Don't call me no mo' King! This ass is no longer yours!" Delishus screamed, walking back to her truck. She got into her car, slammed the door and drove off. Her tires lit the streets on fire, screeching as she peeled away in a crazy spin.

"What?" he asked innocently after watching Delishus drive away. Harmony stared at him, waiting for his response. By now many neighbors and people who knew them, were outside laughing at the fight scene. He was pretty sure a few had taken out their phones and recorded the action.

"You tell me what's up, King. Is she for real? You messing around with her after all those promises you made. Promises of being with me, wanting to marry me and shit? Lying like she was yo' damn cousin! I knew that shit didn't sound right when it came out of your mouth!"

"Come on inside. Marry you? When the hell I say I was doing that? We got enough of our business out here in the streets already. Let's go inside and talk about this," King suggested. But Harmony snatched her elbow away the instant he touched her. He continued to reach out for her while stepping towards the porch. Harmony walked past him, dodging his grasp. She put her hand up to his chest to stop him.

"No, take yo' ass back to where you came from. I'm not going to keep on forgiving you." Harmony said, folding her arms across her chest.

"She lying baby. I promise you there is nothin' going on between us! I know I lied about her being my cousin. That's because I really thought she was until she tried to push up on me. We met on Facebook and she told me she was my family. I saw her the other day and turns out she is just another thirsty ass broad. Delishus has been stalking and calling me like crazy. Don't listen to her. Come on, you know I love you," King told her, kissing her lips unexpectedly.

He put on his puppy dogface and as usual, Harmony gave in. "Okay. But I'm not playin'. If I find out you lyin', I'm gon' cut you out of my life. And I mean that literally," Harmony told him, looking down at his genitals and back at his eyes, letting him know she meant business. King followed her inside and cooked a quick meal, hoping Harmony would forgive him. He needed to make sure Harmony's mother didn't find out or else he'd really be in trouble.

CHAPTER 6

She showered up and wrapped her hair around her head. Once she was done, she slipped on her black halter-top dress that she had just bought from Macy's. While putting on her face, she heard a knock on the door. "Come in," she answered.

"Harmony, did you get those papers signed like we talked about? And when is the wedding?" Her mother, Debra, asked as she entered the room. She took a seat on the bed while puffing on a Newport 100.

"No, I meant to go by the insurance place the other day, but it was closed after I left the mall."

"Look, you are getting beside yourself young lady. If this plan is going to work out like we talked about, then you have to get this ball rolling. What about the wedding? I told you to set a date, that way everything can fall in place," Debra fussed.

"Momma, stop talking to me like I'm a little girl. I said I will handle everything. I am waiting for him to buy the ring." She said in a sassy tone of voice, really not feeling the bullshit idea that her mother was talking about.

"What the hell for? Buy the engagement ring to push for the wedding. His broke ass can't afford to buy anything after just getting out of prison. Step up and take charge. How do you think I was so successful at becoming a widow?" Debra advised.

"Okay. I guess I didn't think about that. But what if he doesn't want to get married so soon?" Harmony asked, sliding her feet into her favorite pair of black Guess sandals.

"It doesn't matter what he wants! Set a date and he will fall in line. Honey, these men don't know what they want. We are women, we have to guide them. Take the reins and steer this horse girl!" her mother whispered as if she was calling a play, the cigarette smoke seeping from her mouth as she spoke.

"Now first things first, go buy a ring. Tell him what day you want to get married. This will be your first marriage so set a close date to get married at the courthouse. Nothing too fancy."

"But it is *my* wedding! I want a traditional one, not a courthouse wedding! I want a fancy gown and my people witnessing me marry the legendary King of the streets," Harmony whined.

Debra rolled her eyes before speaking. "That's how I felt after my first two marriages. Your father was the first to feel my wrath with his cheatin' ass and David was the last. With you and me working together, we can be sitting on a mansion with millions of dollars in no time. Then we can travel from city to city, country to country. I suggest you do as you are told, otherwise you and King will be out on the curb."

Harmony didn't dare disobey her mother. Hearing her confess that she was behind her father's death, confirmed that Debra was nothing more than a cold-hearted bitch! And Harmony could easily be a pawn in her hand as well, if she didn't do as they agreed to do while King was locked up. Debra was about her money and always has been ever since Harmony could remember. She only let King live with them because she knew that it would benefit her eventually.

Bo walked into the house and was surprised that the front door was unlocked. Once he got upstairs, he looked towards King's bedroom in search of him. Once he heard voices coming from the room, he stood on the other side and listened instead of knocking.

"I'll set the wedding for next month and I want one in the backyard, not the courthouse. If we are going to get more money from the life insurance, I may as well splurge how I want to on the wedding so that he can at least think it is for real," Harmony suggested.

"Okay, if that's what you want, then we can try to work some things out. Don't get all worked up, ain't you pregnant?" Debra asked.

Harmony sighed before speaking. "Yeah, but I just hope that King don't suspect nothing. The baby could be here towards the end of the year. I'm only a few weeks, but he might put two and two together."

"Well it doesn't matter. By the time the baby starts to look like its daddy, King will be six feet under. Do you know who the daddy is?" Debra asked blowing out a cloud of cigarette smoke.

"Of course I do, I ain't no hoe or nothing. But I don't know if Tori is ready to be a father. He still acts immature. Even though he and King are family, he is starting to lose his cool. I should have never told him I was pregnant to begin with," Harmony responded as she put on her lip-gloss and popped her lips.

"Shit, the more the merrier. It's actually good that Tori knows he has a baby on the way; then you can work on him next. Girl, you got a two-for-one deal breaker here! Or better yet, we might can get Tori to knock King's ass off since they fuckin' the same pussy. Niggas kill niggas everyday over good pussy out here in these streets. Don't sweat it. Everything will fall in place," Debra said, putting out the cigarette in the empty soda can next to her on the dresser.

Bo's face balled up as if he'd just bit into a Lemon. "Thirsty ass bitches!" he whispered behind the door. He couldn't believe his ears. He'd heard all he needed to hear. He realized he spoke louder than he thought because before he could get down the stairs the bedroom door opened.

"Bo, what are you doing here?" Debra said, surprised at his presence. She prayed he was just walking into the house.

"Hey Deb, I was looking for King. He was going to be on his way home in a minute. Guess I must have beat him here. I'll just wait outside. You sure are looking lovely by the way," he said, cracking a smile while he maintaining his calm demeanor. He continued taking steps down the stairs, rushing out the front door. Debra followed him down the stairs and walked into the kitchen to fix herself some coffee.

"Who were you talking to?" Harmony asked, making her way downstairs.

"Bo was here looking for King. He's outside on the porch. And what happened with you when you called me upset a few weeks ago?"

"Fine time for you to ask. Where were you when I needed you? Some big bitch rolled up to the house, claiming to be sleeping with King! She had me in a headlock and everything! That chick was triple my size. She was bigger than you and me put together," Harmony said, exaggerating the truth of course.

"What? Where is his trifling ass at right now? What the hell is he still doing in my house?" Debra said, becoming more upset at the thought of Harmony not being able to defend herself while she was away. Debra walked over to the window, spotting King outside. She made a mental note to speak with him. "So he likes big girls, huh?" Her eyes were on him, she was watching him like a hawk.

"I guess so. I don't think he really likes her though, momma. He said that she's stalking him or something."

"Girl hush! That nigga lying, ain't nobody stalking his ass. Most men play the victim knowing that they keep up just as much bullshit as the woman sniffing up behind their asses! I am going to have a few words with him. Believe that! He is outside as we speak," Debra said, eyeing King.

"Mama, do not go out there confronting him, then he will know I told you. He hates when people gets in his business," she responded.

"Alright, I'll save my speech for later. I won't tell him you told me." She took a sip of her coffee and walked to her bedroom. She knew just what her next move would be and she couldn't wait.

******

"Brah, I'm telling you they got some real foul shit planned for you. Be careful," Bo warned. He whipped his head around when he heard the front door swing open. He didn't want to tell King what he heard about Tori and the pregnancy, but planned to have a talk with his son later. *How could his family become subjected to such foolishness?* Bo wondered.

"Hey Uncle Bo, how you doing?" Harmony asked, trying to act cordial. He stared at her and shook his head before looking away. Bo lived down the block from them in a house with his wife, Erma. He had three children with her. One of his sons in particular, Tori, took a liking to Harmony while King was away. He sent a quick text to Tori, letting him know that he needed to talk to him. Bo was pretty sure that he had seen Harmony leaving from Tori's house a few times, but he kept that to himself.

"I'm aight. Probably about to head over Tori's house in a minute," he said, staring at her. She offered him a grave expression and King observed the tension between the two of them.

"Oh okay, well I need to talk to King, so if you will excuse us, there's something we need to discuss in private," she said, offering a fake smile.

"I bet you do. Let me tell you this one time and you better listen up good. I don't play when it comes to my family. King may be my nephew, but he is more like my son. If anything happens to him I will hold you responsible since you are condoning this *street* life that you love so much," Bo told her just before walking off.

King knew she was about to say something smart so he decided to play along with Harmony, keeping the details Bo gave him in the back of his mind. "Harmony, what you want to talk about now? I ain't up for no arguing or nothing." They walked into the house with Harmony leading the way. He watched her switch her ass harder with each step she took.

"Who said anything about arguing? I just want you to know how much I love you. I'm going to the jewelry store out at Lenox Mall in a few minutes. Do you really love me like you say?" Harmony asked him as he trailed her to the living room.

"Yeah, what kind of question is that?" He twisted his face up in disbelief.

"Well, I think we should go ahead and get married then. Since we love each other, it's time we make it official. We're not getting any younger. We already got three kids," she told him.

"Three? I ain't got but two children! Where the hell you count another one at?" he asked, puzzled at where she was going with her discussion. *If this bitch tell me she pregnant, I'm just gonna kill myself! Or is she counting another baby out there somewhere? Guess I have been fucking off with those guards real tough,* he considered, allowing his thoughts to tumble in his head.

"Well, I found out yesterday that I am pregnant. So it looks like you are going to be a father again," she said, smiling and wrapping her arms around his neck. She avoided eye contact and kissed his lips.

NOOOOOOO! King screamed on the inside, stunned at the news. *How in the hell does she keep ending up pregnant?*

"If we have another girl, we can name her after me and if we have a boy, we can name him after you. I mean not with the exact same name, but something similar to our names," she said, rubbing her stomach. For the first time, he could actually tell that she had a little pouch. It was nothing like when he saw her the day he got released, but he just figured it was due to her excessive drinking.

"Harmony, we don't need to have any more kids! Didn't you just complain about having money? Enough money so that you don't have to get a job? A baby is the most expensive thing you can have, and definitely another child will hinder us from being able to move forward without you having to find work. We can't have this baby. I can make you an appointment if you want me to," he stated.

"Nigga, I'm not having no damn abortion!" she argued back as he flopped on the couch like his world was coming to an end.

"I ain't playing Harmony! Make the damn appointment! End of discussion!" he advised.

"Okay I will, as long as it is not too late to have one. Can we still get married next month though?" she asked, hoping now that she agreed to go through with the procedure that he would give in to her request.

"We don't have the money for a wedding. Why don't we wait until we have enough money saved up? Then, we can get married sometime next year," he suggested.

"Next year? Kill yo' self for saying some bullshit like that to me. Fuck next year!" she shouted.

Damn, that's exactly what I was thinking about doing! Is this bitch psychic? He thought to himself. "Let me think about it Harmony and I will get back with you on the answer. You said you about to go to the mall so take yo ass on then," he told her lying down on the couch.

"Don't you want to go with me? Come on, we can see if they have that chain you wanted the last time we went inside the jewelry store." The minute she mentioned buying him something, King sprung up from the couch more alert. Anytime a gift for him was up for grabs, he didn't hesitate to do what he needed to do to get it.

"Sho' nuff! Hell yeah! Glad you mentioned that! Come on let's go," he said, taking the keys off the table and leading the way out the door. If he was going to roll with his strategy of undermining Harmony, the least he could do was get everything he could from her at this moment.

CHAPTER 7

Nearly three weeks had passed since Delishus last saw King. Whenever he would come by her apartment, she wasn't there or at least she pretended not to be. He didn't know her schedule or where she worked, which made it even more difficult. On this particular evening, she walked into the deli and ordered a sandwich combo, preparing to enjoy a lunch date with Toya. Especially, since they hadn't done anything together in a while.

"Is this stuff here healthy? I wouldn't want us to ruin the diet we've been working so hard on. Can't you tell I lost almost thirty pounds?" Toya asked.

"Honey, fuck a *diet!* Okay? I need some meat and bread in my life! But yes, I can see it girlfriend. You are looking good too! Can you see the fifteen pounds I've shed over the last couple of weeks? We're making progress, but we can't starve ourselves. Plus, this place is healthy eating too. I used to come here when I was modeling for *Plus* magazine a few months ago," Delishus said, taking a seat at the table.

"Girl you are so crazy! Hell yeah I see the weight loss though; keep on doin' what you're doin'! In no time, we'll be at the weight we want to be. Speaking of modeling, when is your next gig?" Toya asked her, taking a seat across from her.

"I don't know. I just ended one contract and now I'm looking for another one. These people in Atlanta don't pay much for plus size models, so I might need to move somewhere that does," Delishus advised.

"I have to use the bathroom. Get my food when they call our order up," Toya told her, racing to the restroom. They'd been drinking a lot of water, so it didn't surprise her that Toya needed to pee for the fourth time since they first started riding around today. There weren't too many delis in their neighborhood, so they decided to go to the one on the south side. Delishus got their orders from the counter and brought their food to the table. A few minutes later, Toya returned to join her.

"Thanks for getting my food. Now don't think just because we're in this restaurant that you can drop the discussion we were having before we walked in. Tell me more about this dude you've been seeing. He obviously means something to you if you're complaining about him pulling a 'stick n move' on you," Toya stated.

"Do we really have to talk about him?" Delishus whined.

"Yes bitch! Where is he from? I need to meet this man, because I've never seen you worked up like you were when you called me. It our girl's day out. Let's do like we always do. Spill it, give me the tea," Toya told her. Delishus closed her eyes for a second. "I'm listening," Toya said while taking a bite out of her sandwich.

"Damn bitch, can I chew my food up?" Delishus asked, still trying to swallow the mouth full of the sandwich she bit into as well. She covered her mouth to avoid spitting some out.

"Heffa, I've seen you with bigger dicks in yo mouth, you better tell me before I take yo phone and go through it. I bet his name is listed under 'Sweet Dick Willie'," Toya laughed. She made Delishus laugh as well, causing her to choke on her food as she swallowed. The pain caused her to take big gulps of soda to relieve the cough.

"Now see, I can't take yo ass nowhere! Shut up Toya, saying some shit like that while I'm eating," Delishus said, laughing again. "Anyways, I swear this dude got me confused. His name is King and no, that is not his nickname. But he was cool, and I thought I liked him."

"But what? Every time you meet a guy, you let him slip through your fingers with your little insecurities. You gotta stop that shit, Dee!" Toya said, shaking her head.

"It has nothing to do with my insecurities. Hell, he does nothing but tell me how beautiful and pretty I am. The sexual chemistry is incredible and I can't even describe to you the way I felt after we did it each time. But I had a feeling that he was not being honest with me. He never spent the night and last time he rushed out of my house as if he had an emergency. Shit, it was after midnight!" Delishus explained, sipping on her soda some more before biting into her sandwich again.

"Gurl, that wasn't no damn emergency. His ass didn't have a ring on his finger did he?" Toya asked with a smirk.

"Not that I can remember. Nope, now that I think about it, he didn't have on any jewelry other than a gold chain. However, after he left my place he ended up having the car accident, which led me to finding out the truth about who he really was. He's living with his baby momma in the hood out in College Park. She's unattractive and so skinny that I could see her rib cage through her shirt. Her butt is the biggest thing on her ugly ass. She claims they're engaged but, of course, he denied it along with denying the fact that we had something going on. Can you believe he told her ass I was his cousin? Where they do that at?" she said with a slight frown on her face. Her mind was all over the place. She just took a deep breath and tried calming herself down.

"Accident? What happened? And when did you see her? Damn, I hate I work different hours from you, I been missin' all the action!"

"A few weeks ago he left my apartment and got into a collision with another car. After I got his address, I went to his house to check on him, but no one was home. The girl he is messing with pulls up with him in the car and we got into a big fight over him. I tried to rip her hair from her scalp!" Delishus confessed.

"Damn, I wish I could have seen that!"

"I'm glad you didn't. I'm even happier that I haven't seen it on YouTube or World Star. You know I avoid being ratchet whenever possible, but ole girl had it comin', talking crazy about me. I think I got even madder because of the way he was acting."

"That's wild, Dee. I'm up here ringing people up at the grocery store getting paid minimum wage, while you're out here scrapping with bitches! Well, he must have taken off his ring then. The only man that I know who runs out after screwing a broad is the married or engaged-to-be-married kind. Have you ever asked about his other life? Checked his phone for pictures of another woman? I bet he is engaged to her and is trying to have his last good time with you before he is taken off the market. And why in the world did he say you were family? Niggas these days, I swear. They come up with the dumbest shit to say," Toya said.

"Doesn't matter to me. He's been calling me, but I've ignored his calls. I don't have time for games and if he wants to play, he can find someone else. I'm so in my feelings though because I really thought he liked me as much as I liked him," Delishus stated picking some of the lettuce off her sandwich and tossing it on a napkin.

"Don't be frustrated, honey. Everything happens for a reason. Maybe he isn't the one, but you're so ready to find Mr. Right that you assumed he was. How does he look? Is his dick big or nah?" Toya asked, smiling. She glanced up to see Delishus staring at her.

"What? I want to know? You've already told me your other business, so stop acting like you haven't. Let me sip on this tea, honey. You know I don't have any other exciting things going on besides my baby and my man!" Toya added, teasing her.

"He's tall and dark skinned. Like I said, he wears a chain with a 'K' that has diamonds in it. His hair is faded but he has waves. Even though he's a thug, he dresses like he has some common sense. His pants aren't hanging off his ass. And he never wears any of those oversized t-shirts. King is very handsome with his pretty white teeth," Delishus said, giving King's full description. She looked up to see Toya's face and wondered why she was frozen staring at something behind her.

"He got a tattoo of a baby's face on his arm?" Toya inquired.

"Yeah, he does actually," Delishus answered, taking another bite of her sandwich.

"What about a tattoo on his leg with a cross? Does he have that as well?"

"Uh yeah, I think so," Delishus responded nodding her head. "Your ass must be psychic or something. Please tell me you haven't fucked this dude before."

"I haven't! Um, and don't look now, but I believe that's him behind us standing in line," Toya warned.

Delishus turned around despite the warning. Her heart stopped the minute she recognized him. There he was in the flesh, standing next to Harmony who was wearing short shorts with a tank top. This time she was able to see that Harmony had King's name tattooed on her arm.

"What the hell?" Delishus said, beginning to frown.

"Well I'll be damned. Wow! Um, um, um, that is him," she said, shaking her head.

"Who is that woman he's with?" Toya asked.

"That's the chick that he lives with. Guess that answers my question after all. If he wasn't engaged to her, then why is he out with her without the kids? Naw, you know what, let me tell his ass something. I don't appreciate him playing me just to get some ass." Delishus said, getting up from her table. She walked over to them and the minute she locked eyes with Harmony, she could sense steam coming from her ears.

"King!" Delishus stated, catching him off guard, her hands on her wide hips. He did a double take and recognized her only a few feet away.

"Shit!" he cursed to himself. He tried to play it off like he didn't know who she was. He went back to ordering his food from the menu. Harmony stared upside his head before turning to look at Delishus.

"Nigga, you heard me call yo' damn name!" Delishus said, getting closer to them. She was angry and all in her feelings. Toya jumped out of her seat and followed suit, not knowing if Delishus was getting ready to mop the floor with the young lady she saw with the man that was supposed to be hers.

"Who the fuck is that hoe hollering at? She better not start no bullshit up in here!" Harmony stated once Delishus was now standing next to them. The cashier registered the order, giving King his total. King didn't even get a chance to pay because of the argument between both women.

"Hoe? Bitch, I got yo' hoe. If I am such a hoe then why was yo' man writing me love letters while he was locked up? As a matter of fact, he should have come home smelling like my pussy, since he was swimming all up in it every chance he got when he first came home! And if you sucked his dick recently, you should know this pussy tastes good," Delishus said, giving King the evil eye. He was speechless at the ordeal and stuttered his words.

"Baby, I don't know what she is talking about! Just ignore her," King said, hoping Delishus would calm down, or at least recant her statement. He knew both women in one place could be deadly and today seemed like the perfect day for a funeral.

"What the fuck is she talm' 'bout, King?" Harmony asked, punching him in the arm.

"Aye man, you better keep yo hands to ya' self! Don't get clowned in this damn place!" King threatened Harmony.

"Sir, that'll be eleven ninety-five," the cashier said, staring at all of them, hoping they would not cause the other customers to leave the store.

"Hold up!" King shouted, taking his money out of his pocket and paying for his food.

"Naw, ain't no damn hold up! Fuck you, King!" Delishus said, throwing up her hands and walking back to her table to get her food.

"You a real foul ass nigga and I don't even know you. Lose my friend's number, lame!" Toya said. King bit his lip, maintaining himself while he paid for the food. Delishus picked up her food and threw it at King, only to hit Harmony in the process.

"Bitch!" Delishus yelled. Toya threw up her middle finger and stomped out with her.

"Uh uh, no she didn't just get that shit on my clothes!" Harmony said, preparing to run after them. King reached for the change and attempted to grab Harmony but missed the opportunity. She slapped his arm out of the way and headed out of the door to follow Delishus and her friend. By the time she got outside, they were already near Toya's car getting ready to take their seats.

"Ratchet ass people," the cashier mumbled. "Next person in line," he said, carrying on with his shift. Because of the rough neighborhood, he wasn't shocked or surprised at the actions of the women. There have been a few fights at the store. Customers fighting other customers,

customers fighting employees, and even employees fighting other employees!

"Come back here! Don't run, you fat ass cow! You gonna wipe this shit off my clothes. Or better yet, why don't you just lick it off because I know yo' big ass is still hungry!" Harmony stated, approaching the women.

"I got yo' fat ass. It's the same fat ass that yo' man had his tongue in, eatin' my booty like groceries," Delishus laughed. "Yes bitch, all that." And walked back around Toya's car to give Harmony exactly what she needed, a certified ass whoopin' that she was more than happy to sign, seal, and deliver! Delishus wrapped her hands around Harmony's neck and choked her, until King came to break up the two women. Delishus had a grip so strong it took Toya to help King get her to release it. Once Delishus felt that Harmony had had enough, she removed her hands and pushed Harmony back. Harmony held her throat while coughing violently. She ran back to her car and popped the trunk. Delishus and King were arguing so tough that neither of them noticed Harmony had pulled out the pistol.

"That hoe got a gun!" Toya said, tapping Delishus on the shoulder. Toya and Delishus hauled ass back to the car while King held Harmony back trying to talk some sense into her.

"Baby, put the gun down! Are you crazy? You know I'm on parole! This is not the kind of attention I need right now," he warned. Harmony still fired two shots at the car, one of the rounds went straight past the car and the other one ricocheted off the ground and went God knows where. Even though tears clouded her vision. Toya whipped her car out of the parking lot just in time, and raced to get out of the neighborhood. She drove so fierce that she ran a red light and nearly got hit by oncoming traffic.

"King, you got me fucked up if you think I'm 'bout to let you cheat on me with Big Foot!" Harmony said turning the gun on him.

"Harmony, chill out! Security rollin' up now... Get in the car and let's go!" King advised. He took the gun from her grasp and pulled her to the car. She cried the entire way to the car, cursing and yelling at him.

Damn this has been a day from hell! King thought. He could only hope that he could patch things up with Delishus. Deep down inside he didn't want to have her find out about his relationship with Harmony that way. Now he needed to find a way to get her back. And there wasn't anything that he wouldn't do, to get her. He was finally ready to admit that he was actually in love with someone and it wasn't Harmony.

******

She rode in the passenger seat in complete silence, while Toya vented about the run in with Delishus' mystery man. She never predicted this situation and she would be lying if she said she hadn't slipped up and caught feelings for King.

"Did you see the look on ole girl's face? She is crazy as a bat! She must not know that BBWs are in style now," Toya stated, half-laughing, half-nervous.

"Yeah, I know right," Delishus mumbled.

"Honey you almost killed her! Yo' death grip is something else! Glad I'm on yo team! I wish she would have tried to hit you, because I haven't fought a chick in so long! I would have jumped in but shit, seemed like to me you had that motherfuckin' match won! I taught your ass good!" Toya joked. Delishus smiled, but couldn't join in on the laughter due to all the pain her heart felt right now.

"I can't believe he played you like that, talkin' about he doesn't know you! Niggas ain't shit! I swear! I see why he cheating on her with you though, because you got more cushion than her. She doesn't have anything on you honey," Toya said, laughing and turning corners to get back to Delishus' house.

"Well forget him. I can find me another man. Plus, Germane has been blowing me up. Can you believe he sent me flowers the other day? I guess I should have given him a chance instead of thinking I could be with King," Delishus stated.

"You better not be sad over that nigga. Karma is a bitch! Some woman is goin' to come right along and break his heart like he did yours. Don't worry about him! I got a cousin I can hook you up with," Toya advised nearly a feet away from Delishus' apartments.

"I'm not trippin' over him. Dicks come a dime a dozen and that's all he was good for anyway," Delishus said, getting out of the car.

"Are you sure you're going to be okay?" Toya asked, feeling sorry for her friend. Women she knew got played all the time by men. *Where did all the good men go?*

"There's enough men out here for each to have their own woman. Instead, they want theirs and every other man's woman too. Greedy sons of bitches," Toya said. She was lucky enough to find her a good man, but every woman wasn't as fortunate as she was. Delishus had been her girl since high school and she knew all too well about her non-stop drama with the men in her life.

"Ain't that the truth? Well call me tomorrow when you have a chance. I'm about to go in the house and turn my phone off. I don't want to rap with no one right now," Delishus advised her before blowing her a kiss. "Smooches," she replied, waiting for Toya to blow one in return. That's how they always did their goodbyes to one another. She waved her hand, not knowing the chaos King was facing at this very moment. If only she could find a man that really loved her for her. Her weight wasn't the problem, but finding a soul mate was a real task. No one wanted to truly give their heart to her and she wasn't taking anything that wasn't being offered freely.

A few hours later, she heard a knock on the door. "Damn, people love popping up on me. I need to move so no one will know where I stay at," Delishus said, wrapping her body in a towel. She stepped out of the shower and turned the A/C off after catching a chill. She slipped on her house sandals and approached the door.

"Who is it?" she asked. After peeping through the hole, she saw Germane standing on the other side.

Ugh, what does his thirsty ass want now? she thought. "It's me, your secret admirer," he answered.

"Well I have a ton of those, so you will have to be more specific," she said without cracking a smile. After her day of drama at the deli with King and Harmony, she was in no mood for joking.

"Damn, so is it like that? I send you flowers and you immediately disregard my affection and desire to be near you?" he asked. She decided not to hold a grudge with him, considering he was being nice to her and that she never caught him with another woman. Opening the door, she quickly adjusted her attitude, finding him dressed in an expensive black suit. His hair was cornrowed back into neat braids and he wore some designer shades that made him look very sexy. Her nipples got hard and he actually made her moist just thinking about all the naughty things he could do to her. She'd only had sex with him twice, but it was enough times to know he could satisfy her every day if she needed him to.

"Oh hey, did I catch you at a bad time?" he asked. "I can come back later if you need me too."

She smiled.

Germane was always considerate of her feelings and such a gentleman. They met at a club a few months ago and had been trying to make her his woman since that night. No matter how many times she turned him down, he never gave up.

"No, you're okay. Let me put on some clothes real quick. But I would appreciate it if you called before coming over. I could have had another man laid up in here or something." Delishus advised, leaving the door open to allow him to enter the apartment.

"Woman, if you had another man in here, I would for sure catch a murder charge. I refuse to let anyone take what is mine," he said, pulling her in near to him. Her knees began to get weak at his touch. He always had a way with words. She blushed and giggled at his comment. He drew her closer, tracing his fingers on her skin.

"So, I'm yours huh?" She looked up in his eyes and asked.

"That's my goal. A beautiful, sexy woman like you, Delishus, deserves a good man. And I am not being conceited, but here I am," he laughed. She joined in laughing until her towel dropped to the floor.

"Oops," Delishus replied while blushing. With Germane, she didn't feel ashamed of her body, as he'd blessed it in many ways before. His tongue had licked every part of her body.

"Sorry. Guess the cat is out of the bag now," he said while looking down below her waist. That in turn made the both of them burst into laughter.

"You are so crazy! What are you doing here anyways?" she asked, picking up the towel and wrapping it around her again.

"I wanted to take you out tonight. Show you off like I wanted to do the other night before you got sick on me.

But when you didn't answer your phone, I thought something was wrong. You in the mood for Salsa?" he asked.

"Salsa and chips? Nah, I'm not really a Mexican food type of woman."

"Not that kind of salsa, Dee. I want to take you dancing," Germane said while smiling at her misunderstanding.

"I've never been dancing before, doing no Salsa. Only dancing I know how to do is black folk dancing. Bank head bouncing, electric slide, stanky leg, shit like that. But when I hit the floor you better know I shut the club DOWN!" she said, shaking her butt looking back at it, making him laugh.

He became aroused the more she twerked with the towel on. "Delishus, if you don't go put on some clothes, you gonna make me do something real *nasty* to you baby. And I really want to do something tonight. We've never been on a real date," he advised.

"Okay baby, you are so sweet. And I appreciate the flowers you sent. They were really nice. Give me a few minutes and I'll throw on a cute dress," she said, rushing to the bedroom. "As long as you promise to be real nasty with me later on tonight."

"Whatever you want me to do, I will do for you baby, you don't have to worry," he said, singing like R. Kelly. Germane always showed her a good time, so she felt the need to get out tonight and forget about King. Who knows, maybe Germane was meant to be her soul mate after all.

CHAPTER 8: TORN
King

"I ought to go upside yo' motha' fuckin' head for playin' me like that in public. Your ass been really feelin' yourself lately! Had me pay for some shit we didn't even get to eat!" King fussed. He steered them back down the street to drop Harmony off. He'd probably ruined his chances of being with Delishus and that alone had him pissed. Of all the days to see her, he just had to see her when he was out with Harmony again.

"Whatever! Don't try to get off the subject. This is twice that we ran into yo' fat ass side bitch and she gets mad because you're with me! Are you plotting to leave me for her or something?" Harmony asked.

"I'm not getting off the subject. It ain't even like that. This is the second time you've showed your ass in front of people who do not need to be in our business. I ain't marrying no jealous ass woman! I told you she is stalking me. She must have known I would be in that place. I wasn't expecting to see her again. I don't answer her calls or nothing!" King lied.

"How about you stop playin' with my heart and just be real. I want you King and I don't like sharing you with other women," Harmony said, taking out a jewelry box. She opened it, showing him the diamond ring band. He took his eyes off the road for a second, forgetting that he was driving.

Is she proposing to me? he wondered. "What's that?" he asked her.

"King, watch where you going!" Harmony shouted, making him snap out of his trance. He looked up just in time to avoid hitting another car. "I see you still ain't used to being on the road yet. This is a ring for you. Will you marry me?" she asked him.

"Uh wow... I've never had a woman pop the question to me before. Are you serious?" King responded. Of course, he wasn't ready to settle down with her. Truth be told, he really didn't want her at all.

"Yeah, I am for real. We're not getting any younger and I want to show you how committed I am to you," she said smiling, but trying to look sincere at the same time.

For a second King forgot about Harmony and her scheming ways. Then the conversation he had with his uncle reminded him that she couldn't be trusted. If Debra and Harmony were plotting to get him to marry her, then he would have to find a way out from underneath her wing. He decided it was time for him to get focused in the gym. Last week he didn't push himself like he should have, but this time he wasn't going to hold anything back. If he didn't get into boxing, he had a deep feeling that he would die in streets, go back to prison or die fucking with Harmony. And neither one of them was an option. In his mind, she would leave this earth before he would.

"I love you Harmony and I will accept this ring. But you got to work on you, baby. I don't want to be tied down to a woman who doesn't respect my hustle. And not the hustle in the streets, but the one in the ring. I wanna make legit money. What good is making money if you can't live to see it? I can't be a thug *and* a husband."

"So... Is that a yes or a no?" she asked, really ignoring his last statement.

"It's a yes on one condition though. You have to help me get my boxing career on track. From now on there won't be any more negative talk about boxing. I don't say anything to you about what you do, so show me the same respect. It's going to cost money for me to box so you have to support me on whatever I need. You see how Floyd Mayweather got his weight up? Nigga got mansions in damn near every city. That could be us, if you act right."

"Okay, yes sir, is that it?" she asked, holding on to the ring. She placed it on his finger when he nodded his head and they went home. He waited until she was asleep and set off to see about his true woman. He liked his BBW more.

******

He took the ring off, tossing it into the cup holder, got out of the car and went to knock on the door, hoping to find her home. When she didn't answer, he opted to wait outside. An hour passed before he finally saw Delishus, smiling and laughing with a man that was a little shorter than him.

"What the fuck is going on here?" he said aloud, as if he had a reason to be mad at her for moving on with her life. The fact that he had Harmony and just accepted her marriage proposal meant nothing to King. He believed his Uncle Bo about the discussion he overheard and was working to come out on top, regardless of what those two gold diggers had planned.

"Delishus!" King yelled, stepping out of the coupe. She kept walking and turned the key to allow the gentleman to enter. However, he stepped back and allowed her to go inside first and walked in closing the door behind them.

"Did she just take this nigga inside the house and ignore me?" King asked to no one in particular. He didn't need an answer because the moment he walked up to the door he could hear them talking. He knocked on the door hard.

"Who is it?" Delishus answered.

"It's me, King!" He thought about the pistol that he always kept on his the small of his back. *If this lame make one false move, I'm gonna have him wearing a shit bag. Dead as serious.*

"King?" Delishus said, snatching the door opened. She turned around to look back at Germane, giving an awkward smile at King trying to play it off. "Why are you here? Go back to your girlfriend or baby momma, whoever she is to you. I told you I don't take playing with my emotions lightly. You've made your bed; now lay in it over there with her."

She attempted to close the door, thinking their conversation was through. "Wait a minute dammit!" he said, pushing back on the door. King was strong, but he only liked to use it in the ring or towards other niggas.

"No, you don't get a minute. I have company. Go away!" She said, now getting a higher pitch in her tone.

"Is everything alright?" Germane asked, getting up from the recliner. He made the mistake of walking over to the door. King got in his face, pushing past Delishus.

"Hell nawl everything ain't aight, pimp! I want you out my ole lady crib right now! She made a mistake by going anywhere with you," King said. He tried to hold his composure as much as he could and realized he sounded lame as hell, just like Jody in the movie Baby Boy; however, he felt the anger rising by the second and that wasn't important now. Germane gave a smile and a light laugh at his comment and waited for Delishus to respond.

"King, get out! I went out on a date with my friend and we would like some privacy, thank you," she said, stepping between the men. "Germane, I apologize; this is someone who I used to date before I met you. Seems now that I am no longer entertaining his lies, he wants to interfere with my life. Give me a second, I'll be right back," Delishus said, taking King by the arm and leading him to the door.

"What? So, you throwing me out? How you gonna choose that nigga over me?" King asked. His feelings were truly crushed, but he had to see it coming. A sexy woman like Delishus wouldn't stay single for too long. They stepped outside, leaving Germane to sit back on the couch near the door so he could ear hustle. He ran his fingers across a photo of Delishus and licked his lips.

"Just give up the act. When you're ready to be the man I need in my life then you can come back. But for now, just leave me alone! I can only be a real bitch for you, boo, not a side bitch," Delishus said, walking back inside the apartment and shutting the door in his face.

"But—" he began to protest. She wasn't hearing it though. She returned to Germane with King still in the back of her mind. She hoped she made the right decision by showing him that she didn't take nonsense. For now, this was the best solution she could come up with to get King out of her system. Still, deep down inside she had strong feelings for him.

CHAPTER 9: WHO DO YOU LOVE

DELISHUS

He knocked on her door. The minute Delishus opened it to his gorgeous smile, her heart began to melt. She smiled while stepping aside to let him in. Normally she went out on several dates before she invited men back to her place, but for some reason she trusted King.

"Hey gorgeous mommy," he said walking in and giving her a hug.

"Thank you. Hope my directions weren't bad," she stated, cracking another smile.

"Nah, they were just fine. I used the GPS on my phone. Nice apartment you have. I don't want none of your boyfriends popping up so let them know that I am here," King joked.

"Whatever. That is not a problem because the men I talk to have no clue where I live," Delishus said, closing the door. She had already prepared a nice meal for them.

"Dinner will be ready in a second," she added, walking into the kitchen.

"That's cool. I just wanted to see you again. I'm glad to hear you know how to cook. I love a woman who knows her way around the kitchen."

"What types of foods do you like to eat? Judging by your stomach, I can tell you ain't missin' no meals," Delishus teased. She poked King in his stomach but ran her fingers up to his chest, giving him a tingling sensation.

"I'm not picky really. Hell, I'll eat yo' ass up and be just as satisfied," he flirted. Delishus continued stirring the mashed potatoes and turned off the cooktop.

"Well, I'm a whole lot of woman. You can't just eat me up in one serving. Come sit down at the table, I'll fix you a plate." She was smiling and showing off her pretty white teeth.

"Thank you," King said, admiring her home décor and small, but cute apartment. *"Nice place you have here. You got any kids?"* he asked.

"Thanks. No, I do not. Can't you tell? The carpet is clean and there are no toys around. What about you? Do you have any?" she responded, bringing him a plate of pot roast with seasoned vegetables and a glass of red wine.

"Yeah, I have two. Boy and a girl...Kaden and Kamil. I try to be the best man I can be to raise them right. I want more kids in the future though. Do you want any kids? My genes are really good. We can make some pretty babies," he teased.

Delishus laughed before answering. "I want a couple, but I'm afraid that if I get pregnant I will blow up like a house and never lose the weight I gain. I have two brothers and their wives showed me all I needed to see concerning pregnancies. Surgery scares me, so if I ended up having a C-section I would probably die at the thought. And I don't doubt that you would make some gorgeous children. Where's their mother at?" Delishus stated, taking a seat with her plate and drink, joining King at the table. She wanted to look him directly in the eye when he gave this answer.

"She lives in the city. We talk from time to time and have a good relationship as far as the kids, but I'm a single man. She does her own thing and I do mine," King advised.

"Very well then. Let's make a toast to a nice evening," Delishus said, raising her glass and connecting with his. His smile was rather brief. They sipped wine and dug into their food. Half an hour later, they were rolling around on her bed getting familiar with one another's bodies.

"Do you have a condom?" she asked. He stopped kissing her neck for a moment and reached into his pocket.

"Yeah, but not that I intended on using it or nothing," he said, hoping not to appear as if he came over her house with sex on the brain.

"Well thank goodness you brought it because I don't have unprotected sex. Go ahead and put it on," she replied, taking a moment to pull down her shorts, *carefully rolling them down her thick curvy thighs*

"You didn't have any panties on?" he asked.

"No, I hate wearing them. If my butt didn't jiggle as much without them, I wouldn't bother wearing any in public," she laughed.

"My type of woman," he responded, pulling down his pants. She saw his semi-erect penis and got excited, knowing he didn't lack in that department at all. She has had a few incidents where the men she slept with weren't worth her time and she hoped this occasion was different.

King knew he was working with a strong nine-inch piece of meat with the curve that most women couldn't resist on sight. He slipped his bulge into the condom without wasting any more time. She reached out to massage him and found him continuing to grow. He slid down a little and removed her bra, taking the time to suck on her breasts. Her nipples got harder and her juices were already beginning to drip. She rubbed on her clit, getting it ready for him, not knowing that he was the type of man who specialized in giving woman oral pleasure as well. King trailed his tongue down her stomach, to the opening between her thighs. He removed her hand and gently sucked on her clit. It swelled instantly and poked out at him, throbbing for more of his tongue. When he stuck his tongue inside of Delishus, he circled her slit and flicked it repeatedly until she began moaning and running her hands all over him. After a few seconds of teasing, he felt her cum, but that wasn't enough. She gripped the back of his head and shook from the magical feeling that overtook her body.

"You like that, baby?" he asked.

She nodded her head as he lifted his. Without expecting any oral pleasure in return, he spread her legs wider and went straight for her G-spot like a lion in the jungle going in for the kill on his prey. Her walls were tight and he could feel himself reaching spots she hadn't had touched before. King took the liberty of pounding her and then slowing down his rhythm, looking down at the thick white cream she'd covered him with. Delishus was going insane from the energy and passion she got from him. The way he moved his body and filled her up, brought out emotions that she never had for any man before. Then she squirted long and hard.

"Damn King, what are you doin' to me?" she moaned.

She dug her head back into the pillow and gripped the sheets. She could feel herself about to explode again but she didn't want to cum before him, so she tried to hold back.

"I'm making you love me, and not just the dick," he responded, finally catching his breath. Drips of sweat fell onto her as he put in work and overtime on her ass. "Turn around," he said in a rough, demanding tone of voice, stopping his flow. She did as she was told and got on all fours, bending over in the bed. This was his favorite position. He loved seeing a woman's ass bounce whenever he dove into her from behind. King placed his hand on her back and wrapped one hand around her shoulder. Once he got in it, he slammed his penis in her as if she had no back walls to be hit. The rougher he got with her, the more she loved it. She moaned and screamed his name. She was no longer able to keep from having an orgasm *and in fact came twice unexpectedly. A couple times, he even heard her say this was HIS pussy. And that definitely made him feel like the King he was! He grabbed her neck and fucked her harder as he was on the verge of releasing. King finally burst into the condom and felt his body jerk. He let out a growl type of moan himself. Thinking how good and tight her pussy was, making him shake his head. He wiped sweat from his forehead and pulled out of her wetness even though he wanted to stay in it all night. Delishus gathered herself after a few minutes and retrieved a towel for him to wipe his sweaty body off. She turned on the shower and kissed him again.*

"I have to get going, but thank you for everything sweetheart. I'll call you when I make it home," he told her while kissing her. She returned the kiss and smiled, nodding her head. That was the first time King made love to her and she would never forget it.

"Miss, your food is ready. That will be twenty dollars," the Korean woman said to her. For a second, Delishus forgot that she was in the food restaurant while fantasizing about her first time with King. She was soaking wet between her legs at just the thought of him.

She smiled and handed the money to her. "Thank you!" she said, walking out of the store. For the last few days, it had been peaceful and stress free. She wanted to keep it that way. Germane was making sure she had everything she wanted. Tonight she wanted to get out and party though, so she dialed Toya to see what she was doing. She pressed the button to unlock her Chevy Avalanche.

"Toya!" she said once her friend answered from the other end.

"What's up, girl? What are we doing tonight?" Toya asked.

"I don't know but I am feeling a girl's night out. Let's go to the Velvet Rope," she suggested.

"Okay I'm down," Toya responded.

"Cool, I'll meet you there. You won't believe what happened to me yesterday when I went out on a date with Germane," Delishus told her.

"Girl, hold it until we get together. I'll get ready now and see you there in a couple hours," she replied. Delishus agreed and disconnected the call. She drove down the street, getting a text from Germane saying that he missed her and couldn't wait to see her again. She smiled and attempted to respond but frowned once King's name flashed on her screen. Tempted not to answer him, she clicked IGNORE. He called right back, despite her declining his call.

"Boy, if you don't quit calling my damn phone! What you want?" she answered.

"Baby, please forgive me! I am so sorry if I hurt you. I never meant to. I really like you Delishus. In fact, I think I love you and I want to be with you. Every day, all I do is think about you. Just give me some time to end what I have with my baby mama then I will be all yours," King rambled.

"I don't know about that King. I have strong feelings for you too, but you cut me pretty deep. A wound like the one you gave my heart, takes time to heal." She was already getting emotional and tried desperately not to let King suck her back into his games.

"Trust me baby, I know how you feel. But if you will give me another chance, I promise I can leave her alone and be there with you. My kids are all I care about and she's threatened to take them away from me if I ever fuck with another woman. Please just don't shut me out of your life, okay? I can't take it," King confessed. He was laying it on thick, but he was so serious about his feelings for her.

The sincerity in his voice and him saying that he loved her, made her soften up a little bit. She sent a text to Germane before responding. "We'll see King. But you better believe that I'm still going to date other people. I am not your woman; therefore, you cannot tell me who I can talk to or where I can go with them. And this time we are going to do things my way. It doesn't matter when you decide to end things with her because, in my eyes, you will always have dealings with her because of your children. I see firsthand that you can say one thing and do another. When I am ready to be serious with you, I will let you know. Until then I am fair game for any man right now," she advised.

"Okay, that's fair enough. But don't expect me to not be jealous if I see you with another nigga. I really like you, Dee, and you know it. Call me when you have time. I'll be waiting to hear from you," King said, ending the call.

******

They parked beside each other after getting to the club early. They wanted to beat the crowd and Toya only had a babysitter for a of couple hours. Delishus had on her black skirt and shimmering top to match her silver wedges. The weather was just right and her flipped curls blew in the wind. As usual, her makeup was beat and she made men stop to stare. Toya wore a red dress with silver pumps. They giggled at the men who gawked at them or whenever a guy made a gesture about their fashionable appearance.

"Two fine ass, big women um, um, um," the door security guard stated once they walked up and handed him their IDs to verify their ages. They both replied with a "Thank you" and entered the building, checking out the scene. They went to the bar until a place to sit became available. After spotting a booth, they took their seats, preparing to order their drinks.

"Girl, this Cosmo is giving me life!" Toya advised, shaking her head to the music.

"Well let me tell you about my life," Delishus replied.

"Aw shit, what happened, honey. Yo' ass should write a damn book! All the bullshit that happens to you is so unreal. I'll write it if you don't want to. Or you can get a ghostwriter or something because you know my grammar ain't right."

Delishus laughed. "Toya, I'm not dealing with you right now. Listen, after we left from seeing King and his girl, tell me why this fool started blowing up my phone, hitting me up on Facebook and sending me texts all day. It was like he was stalking me now that he got caught. I don't understand him."

"I hope you told his no good ass to lose yo' number!" Toya interrupted.

"I ignored him, thinking he would take the hint. When I tell you this fool popped up at my house while I was out with Germane, I was so shocked!"

"What? Get out of here!" Toya said, bucking her eyes.

"No, I'm not lyin'. Like, I don't understand. Dudes want to do whatever, and expect women to just take it," Delishus said, sipping on her drink.

"What did Germane do?"

"He stood his ground and appeared calm. It was King who I was worried about. He acted like he wanted to rip Germane a new asshole. He was instantly jealous," Delishus said, laughing.

"Chick, you have to watch for stuff like this. I see women on TV all the time saying 'he started out nice and shit, then I don't know what happened' when the dude becomes a certified nut job over them, landing him in jail!"

"King has been in jail and prison before already."

"Oh my God, Delishus, stop talking to him. He is making me nervous. You may have to move if he keeps on coming over without you knowing. Damn shame you have to start doing background checks on these men before you can start taking them serious. Then again, you like them thugged out ass niggas anyway," Toya said, taking a sip from her drink. She looked over to the left, spotting a familiar face. She nudged Delishus to follow her eyes.

"Damn, can't I go one week without seeing King or his damn slut?" she said in frustration. Harmony gyrated to the music and clapped her hands, while laughing at a few females that did the same around her. Guess everyone needed a night out tonight.

"That trick can't even dance, let's go shut the floor down before we leave." Delishus said, finishing her drink.

Toya downed hers as well, not wanting to take it to the dance floor. She knew her and Delishus liked to wiggle freely without having to worry about wasting any drink. They made their way to the dance floor and began popping their phat, round asses to the music. After a few minutes of putting on a good show, Delishus and Toya gained the crowds attention. They couldn't see how two woman of their sizes were making their asses clap and breaking it down to the floor as if they were just as little as the skinny chicks. Delishus waved her hands in the air rotating her hips, as a gentleman walked up behind her, following her rhythm. Toya danced as well, clapping to the beat while she bent over and shook her ass on a cute guy who joined her.

"Look at those big girls getting down over there!" Savannah stated laughing at the scene. She found it comical that they were bringing attention to themselves.

"They may be big, but they are moving! Look at how she's twerking on him!" Harmony said. Once she realized it was Delishus, she got upset. "I'm ready to go. This place is whack as hell!"

Delishus and Toya noticed all eyes on them. They soon saw dollar bills falling on them and looked up to see where they were coming from. Men and women were standing around them watching but there were three in particular that had money in their hands. They were making it rain on the ladies as they did their thing. This made Toya start feeling herself and she immediately stepped up her game dropping down into a split. People in the crowd cheered them on and danced to the music. Harmony walked past them, mugging the two women. Delishus gave her a smirk while continuing to dance. She kept her eye on Harmony just in case she wanted to get physical. Toya jumped up and started back dancing. They had the time of their lives that night but Delishus' joy came to an end when Germane called her ruining her vibe.

"Hey baby!" she answered.

"Where are you? What is all that noise in the background?" he asked her.

"I'm at the Velvet Rope with Toya. We should be leaving here soon."

"You didn't tell me you were going out tonight. If we are going to be together, you are going to have to stop acting like you're single. Make this your last night of partying!" he warned.

"Um excuse me, but the last time I checked, I was grown. We're out having fun. I ain't acting like I am single. I haven't given my number out to anyone so chill out."

"You haven't given your number out but you sure as hell have been letting men feel up on you!" Germane said with anger in his tone.

"No I have not. Why are we arguing? I said I will call you later, bye!" Delishus said hanging up in his face. Germane walked up to Delishus and pulled her by her arm.

"What the hell!" she said, caught off guard that he was already in the club, even though he acted like he didn't know her location. She was more upset that he was treating her like she was his woman even though they weren't official.

"I said I want you out of this club, bring your hot ass on!" Germane told her. Toya finally noticed what was going on when she saw Delishus snatch her arm from him. She stopped dancing and followed behind them.

"Where are you goin, Dee?" Toya asked.

"Toya, this is Germane; Germane meet my best friend Toya," Delishus stated.

"Nice to finally meet you. I have heard a lot about you," Toya advised, reaching out to shake his hand.

"Yeah, I wish I could say the same. Anyways, Delishus, I don't want you dancing with these other men. I think it's real disrespectful," he said, declining to shake Toya's hand. His face looked familiar but Toya couldn't quite figure out where she saw him before.

"I don't like your attitude mister!" Toya said in a drunken slur.

"Please mind your own business! This is between me and my woman," Germane said, getting an attitude. His eyes turned into slits.

"Don't talk to my friend like that! And I am not your woman!" Delishus interjected, putting her finger in his face as they made way towards the door to exit. With Germane embarrassing her, Delishus didn't even want to dance or party anymore. She was shocked at his behavior and pissed that he'd clowned her in front of Toya.

"Yes you are! We have been on plenty of dates and I have committed myself to being the perfect gentleman for you. Now go home and stop acting like a hoe!" he ordered once they finally reached the parking lot.

"If I am hearing you correctly, you don't like your woman to be out in the clubs, right?" Delishus responded.

"You damn right I don't!" he answered.

"Well check this out. I am not your woman, girlfriend, or whoever you think I am. Since we obviously can't see eye to eye, then we should call our little friendship over and done with! I will not let any man control me or tell me what to do," Delishus said, walking to her car. Toya watched them argue and pulled out her keys to unlock her car. She text messaged her boyfriend to let him know she was on her way home.

"No, we will not end it like this. Hold up," he said only a few steps behind her.

"No, leave me alone! I can admit that I should have told you where I was going, but you don't own me. I am free to go where I please! If this is the way you treat your woman, then we are definitely not going to work out. This conversation is over with!" Delishus barked at him while getting into her car.

"Damn, bad first impression to make on me. You know you have lost all your cool points," Toya said, shaking her head getting into her car. He stood there in the parking lot dumbfounded. Delishus and Toya drove off heading in the directions of their homes. Germane was sure that they would talk about tonight's fiasco.

"This bitch done straight tried me like a real fuck nigga.

Like it's that simple," he said aloud, walking back to his car. Germane left the parking lot driving like a maniac. But he was far from done with Delishus in his opinion. His madness was just getting started.

Chapter 10: *King*

She bit into her apple before bending over to suck on the juices in his ear. Harmony's mother reached under the covers to squeeze his dick. As mad as she was right now, he better be glad she didn't shoot him in it. This was the best way she felt she should wake him up from his slumber. King sat up quickly and gasped when he saw her ugly face.

"Ouch," he said with a frown. "What was that for Debra?" He was staring at her now with his face twisted.

"My baby girl came to me worried because of one of your tramp ass side bitches. This is the last time you make my Harmony shed another tear for your *sorry* ass! Honestly, I don't know what she sees in you. Aside from being pleasing to the eyes, you don't have a damn thing going for yourself. Have your things out of my house by this weekend!" Debra ordered finally releasing his manhood. She took the liberty of applying pressure to the head just to get her point across.

"Shit! That hurts! Please don't kick me out, Harmony already forgave me and I promised her that I didn't do anything wrong," King tried to convince her.

"Well this is my house. You don't work, clean, or take care of my needs or your kids, so why should I let you stay? If you cannot abide by my rules, then goodbye," she said, getting ready to walk away. King slammed his eyes shut, cursing himself for what he was about to do.

"Wait...okay... What do you want, Debra?" he asked.

"I'm not sure. Your broke ass doesn't have too much to offer," she replied.

"If it ain't one thing it's another," King said, biting down hard on his bottom lip. He followed Debra's eyes down to his manhood. King knew the power of the D so he grabbed his dick hiding his prize possession. "This can't be what you want," he said, praying that he didn't have to do the unthinkable with Harmony's mother.

"Maybe it is. I've heard people say *broke* dick, is the *best* dick. So show me what you're working with, and we'll see if we can cut a deal. I need to see what has my daughter going crazy. Plus, I hear you like woman with a lot of meat on their bones," Debra stated, walking up and pushing him back onto the bed. She straddled King and began rubbing his bare chest. He looked up at the clock, realizing that Harmony would be at the hair salon during this time. If he ever wanted to pull off a trick with her mother, now was the time because she always spent hours at the salon gossiping.

"Wait a minute. Harmony will kill me if she finds out," King said, hoping that would make her fall back. But Debra didn't let up; she stood back up and pulled down her pants, exposing her underwear.

"If you wanted a BBW all you had to do was say so," she uttered, flicking her tongue at him.

This bitch got on certified granny panties! Talkin' about a BBW... shit, she looks more like a BUB, Big Ugly Bitch! King snickered to himself. He stared at the different color flowers imprinted on Debra's sagging, white panties, but it was a phat Camel toe print in front.

"What's so funny?" she asked him.

He shook his head and wiped the smirk off his face. Not only did she have on big drawers, but she also had a bush of hair so thick between her legs that it looked like she hadn't shaved in years. She scratched her curly pubes making King want to throw up. Everything about her was unattractive and a huge turn off.

"Nothing, I just can't believe that I'm doing this. Don't you feel bad for even wanting to sleep with yo' daughter's fiancé?" he asked her. Not wanting to get caught up, King walked over to retrieve a condom.

"Why should I? Everything in this house belongs to me, including you. You just make sure you keep this between us," Debra said. He turned around spotting her legs sprawled open waiting to receive him. He took a shot from the bottle of Jack Daniels that rested on the nightstand, hoping that it would make his situation easier.

Harmony's mother was twice as ugly as she was with her big crooked nose and fish eyes. She had long black hair and weighed just as much as Delishus, if not more. Debra was a tall, big woman with a body like a seal. And so out of shape that even Dr. J's Curves couldn't bring her back. She was known for seducing men until they became her husband. She would empty out their bank accounts and be done with them once they were broke. King couldn't understand who would even want to be with her, let alone make her their wife.

"Trust me, no one will ever hear a word of this. As a matter of fact, I don't even want to remember having done this," he said.

"Get yo' ass over here boy! You are wasting my time," she said, getting antsy. She rotated her butt on the bed and she juggled her breasts at King, attempting to display her most seductive look.

"I hope I am having one horrible dream," King whispered. He took the last sip of alcohol before making his way over to Debra. He couldn't dwell on his betrayal of Harmony, his livelihood was at stake. King swore to himself that this would be the first and last time he had sex with any woman other than Debra, for money. He had a reason for doing what he was doing, but it still didn't make him feel any better. When he pushed his pipe in her he did it so rough and out of anger he thought that she would make him come out, but instead she gasped and begged for him to go deeper. *Big pussy bitch ain't got no grip or no bottom*, King thought to himself while shaking his head.

******

Trying to forget about his morning nightmare with Debra, King set off to go to the gym. The smell of her Liz Taylor perfumed proved his nightmare was anything but a dream. He drove down the street in Debra's Lincoln LS, making sure he stopped at every stop sign and red light. The entire way he thought about his life as he passed other urban neighborhoods. He thanked God he was out of them, but could feel himself slipping back. He missed the money, the drugs, and the fast life he'd become accustomed to since the age of sixteen. Being on the straight and narrow didn't compare to his past life. King used to run the streets as a teenager fighting, stealing, selling crack, pulling of robberies and even killing if he had to. His mother passed years ago from breast cancer and his father died not long afterwards from a stroke. His uncle Bo tried to help as much as he could, but there was only so much that he could do. King's mind was going in all directions, but he wanted money. He wanted to be free from all this drama that he was caught up in and so damn fast that he didn't know how it happened. He woke up to his baby mama's mama holding his dick and then he got blackmailed to fuck her. All he could do was shake his head at the thought of it all.

King felt a tap on his shoulder bringing him back into reality. "What up pimp!" his uncle Bo said, greeting him.

Bo was his mother's twin brother. Every time he saw his uncle, it reminded him of his mother, Viola. She did her best to raise King, but he followed in his father's footsteps by becoming a drug dealer. His first run-in with the police came when he aided some boys on a snatch and grab store robbery somewhere in East Atlanta. He was caught and sent to a juvenile detention center. They released him, and King did well for a while. But then a couple years later, he got into a fight at a bar when a dealer tried to short him some money. Of course, he paid a good lawyer to have a low sentencing so his time in juvenile didn't last long.

"Aye, don't be sneaking up on me like that. Might catch one of these fists to yo' jaw," King said, taunting him with his balled up fist. Bo dodged playfully as if he was preparing to be hit.

"Whatever, you missed two days of workout, so I don't have to worry about you hittin' me too hard," Bo joked. They walked over to the other side of the gym and noticed a couple white men sparring.

"Excuse me, but this is normally my area of the gym around this time. You mind taking your session over to the other side?" King asked the two gentlemen.

Tye, a gym employee, was familiar with King and stopped what he was doing. The other unfamiliar guy continued swinging without regards to King's statement.

This only made King more upset. He was already frustrated and was looking for something or someone to take his anger out on. He walked over to the gentleman noticing that his punches were heavy and hard. But King felt he could take the guy down if he wanted to. They were the same height and close on the scale.

"You can't hear? I said move before I move you myself," King told him. Bo tapped King on his arm, grabbing his attention. "What?" he shouted, turning to face his uncle.

"Step off boss man. You don't want to see those kinds of problems," Bo warned. King chuckled before speaking.

"I ain't scared of nobody. What kind of problems can he possibly give me that I can't handle?" King asked. He got his answer when he turned around only to see a red gloved fist inches from his face. The strange man punched King, knocking spit from his mouth. King began to taste blood as he sucked his teeth.

"Did you just hit me?" King said, rushing to the man's face. It was obvious that he had met his match when the guy threw another punch. King ducked this time and began alternating a couple swings in his direction. After a couple seconds, their fight turned into an unintended sparring session, as both men threw punches while dodging the other's counter attack.

"Damn, you're pretty good," the guy stated. "I'm Dino. I meant no disrespect. We can do this all day if you want, but it's not going to get us anywhere. This is my first time at the gym, but I wasn't expecting to end up in a fight. Just blowing off some steam," Dino stated.

"Whatever. You caught me off guard. Don't try to talk yourself out of this ass whooping you're about to get," King said. Bo and Tye stared at them, hoping they wouldn't tear up the gym.

"Yo', you got real anger issues. Would be better if you showed that aggression in the ring. You could make some real money that way," Dino told him. King stopped for a second and took heed to what he was saying.

"I ain't gonna lie, you are pretty good with yo' hands too. What made you come here? You do realize you on the West side of Atlanta, don't you? Niggas ain't fightin' out here in the streets," King said to him. They stepped in front of a punching bag a few feet away.

"King, you're wasting time. Are we goin' to work out or not?" Bo asked.

"Is that your dad?" Dino asked.

"Nah, that's my uncle. He's become my personal trainer though," King replied before turning around to respond to Bo. "Give me a minute," King said in Bo's direction, throwing up his hand.

"What are you training for? Fighting some old man on the streets or something?" Dino asked. King looked at him with raised eyebrows.

"Ah, I see you got jokes too. No more fightin' in the streets for me. I just told you lil niggas got big guns out there. I've been itching to get in the ring professionally and I hope to get in shape for an upcoming match. I'm waiting for Uncle Bo to get me into a tournament. Bo is the only man who believes in me," King admitted while adjusting the punching bag to an acceptable position.

"Well, my dad used to be a boxer back in the day. He taught me a few things before he died from a heart attack. Come show me what you got," Dino told him.

King hesitated at first. Especially, since it had been a while before he put his trust in another man besides his uncle. Most of the people he used to hang out with were either dead or in jail. Boxing became his second love after his love for the streets.

"Cool. Aight then," King said, taking a few swings at the solid bag. He grunted with every throw. The bag moved left and then right. Dino grabbed hold of the bag, bringing it to a stop. He let King continue punching until he got tired.

"Okay, okay. Nice arm movement, but you have to make sure you are hitting key areas. There are certain parts of the body that make for perfect targets of destruction. Let me show you," Dino told him, stepping around to the other side. King stood back and watched Dino give furious blows to the upper and bottom as well as the left and right side of the punching bag with powerful left and right hooks, jabs here and there. His hands were quick as lightning with every swing. His combinations were sick! King was definitely amazed at what he saw.

"Uncle Bo, I think I just found me a new workout partner," King said, turning around to trade glances with his uncle and Tye. They both gave him a thumbs up in approval. All King could think about now was being in a ring. Dino was his golden ticket to helping him out of the hellhole that he ended up in by being with Harmony. Only problem was, King didn't know if he could trust Dino. It didn't matter right now though, with a white boy in his corner, he knew his possibilities of becoming a success were only about to get greater.

CHAPTER 11

After a couple hours at the gym, Dino and King agreed to meet each other for lunch. They found a nice table inside of the lounge to chill at. Considering all Dino knew about boxing, King figured it was best to get to know a little more about him. He could tell he was a smart man and realized that people took you more seriously when you had a white man to vouch for you. It had been months since King reached out to the association for boxing, but he still hadn't heard back from them yet.

King's phone rang before he got the chance to order his food. "Hello," he answered.

"Where you at?" Harmony asked from the other end.

He could hear Kevin Gates' "I Don't Get Tired" blasting in the background.

"I'm out eating, what's up?" he answered in aggravation. She stayed trying to keep tabs on him, which annoyed him to no end. What she didn't know was that he was always two steps ahead of her. She already lacked trust in him, thanks to Delishus, so he knew his meeting with Dino would show her that he was trustworthy.

"Nothing, I just came home. Why did you leave dishes in the sink? Momma hates when you do that. Then I have to come here to clean the shit up!" Harmony complained in her nagging ass voice.

Dino raised an eyebrow after placing his order. The waitress waited patiently until King was ready to make his. He studied the menu a second while blowing out hot air. Having to explain himself in front of Dino was a bit embarrassing. Not only was Harmony making him glad that he slept with Debra, but she was also motivating King to make some good business with Dino.

"Gimme the lemon pepper wing special with loaded fries. And bring me a Heineken. Thanks," King told the waitress.

"Who the hell are you talking to? Better not be wining and dining no bitch with my money!" Harmony warned.

"Man, chill with all that shit. I'm in a business meeting. I'll call you once I leave," he told her. She hung up the phone without responding back. King rolled his eyes and put his phone down. The waitress took their menus after Dino ordered and left the two men in privacy.

"Business meeting, huh?" Dino asked.

King nodded his head. "Yeah, if that's alright. My circle is small and I like to keep it that way. The only reason I agreed to meet here is because I think I have an offer to make," he replied.

"What type of offer?" Dino asked.

"Well since boxing comes natural to you, I was thinking maybe you could help me out. I won't take up much of your time, but if you can spare a few days in the gym training me, I promise it will be worth it."

"My time is very valuable, King. What's worth spending a few hours a day or like you say, spending a few days in the gym to teach you anything?" Dino inquired.

"When is your next shift, Dino?" the waitress asked once she reached the table to bring them their drinks.

"Hey Tina, I'm on schedule for tomorrow. Thanks," Dino said, taking the drinks and preparing to return to the most important conversation at hand.

"Cool. I work tomorrow as well. Wanna catch a bite to eat before you come in?" Tina asked, handing King his beer while popping the top off it.

"No thanks, Tina. I have some business to take care of. Maybe some other time." Dino told her. King could see the look of disappointment on her face as she nodded her head and walked away.

"I work here at the bar some nights," Dino explained, sensing that King would be questioning the odd behavior between the two of them.

"But shawty was flirting with you, batting her pretty eyes and shit. Why didn't you jump up on that man?" he joked. They both stared at Tina's ass while she walked towards the back of the bar.

"Tina is old news. Throwback Thursday. I hit that one time when I was angry with my girl, and now she's trying to be more than just a friend. I've been dodging her calls all day," Dino explained.

"With an ass like that, she can be anybody she wants to me!" King told him, watching Tina's petite frame switch with each step. Her heels elevated her butt, making it perkier than it really was. King never dated outside his race but there was a first time for everything.

"What type of woman you have that will make you hit and quit that?" he asked Dino.

"The type of woman that makes you fall in love with just hearing the sound of her voice. She has you wanting to cook breakfast for her in the middle of the night. I don't know, I can't explain it. I feel like she's my soul mate," Dino said. The way he talked about this chick proved that he was head over heels for her.

"Well, after hearing all of that you know I got to ask why you cheated on her then. What did she do? Sleep with one of yo' homeboys?" he asked.

"She's the one who broke up with me. For some reason she ended up finding another man who treated her better I guess. She said I never liked to do anything or go anywhere. But I don't like clubs and partying. Considering Tina's situation, there was no way we could ever be a real couple anyway. She's a married woman," Dino confessed.

Tina walked up, sliding out plates of food to both of them.

"Need anything else?" she asked. King could tell her question was directed more towards Dino, who shook his head and said his grace. King on the other hand acted like he had lost his manners, digging into his food rather quickly. Tina's smile faded away once Dino acted unfazed by her presence. The two men definitely had more in common than they thought.

"Whoa! Talk about cold-hearted. Any reason why you don't plan on hitting that again? If your old lady pumped the brakes on your relationship, then why not move on. It's plenty of women out here," King stated.

"Because, I want to be free for a minute. I need to get myself together. Plus, I'm scared to jump into anything serious with another female right now when I don't know if it's really over between me and my ex. Why you asking so many questions about my love life? I heard someone on the other end of your phone who did not sound happy to hear you were out," Dino said, taking a bite into one of his wings. King didn't get a chance to answer when his phone rang again. He looked at the screen, but this time it was Delishus who was calling.

"Hol' up," he told Dino holding up a finger. "Hey baby," he answered.

"I need to talk to you," Delishus stated.

He checked his watch and noticed that it was approaching five o'clock in the afternoon.

"Okay, about what? You've already said everything you needed to say. I told you to give me a little time. I can swing by later if you want me to, but I'm in a business meeting right now. I'm working on getting some things going on in the ring," King told her. King really liked her and he knew that he needed to prove himself worthy of her. She was tired of his lies and he didn't want to lose her behind the games that he kept playing.

"This is a serious matter, King. I think I'm pregnant," Delishus blurted. She knew he wasn't the type of man to go off hearsay and she had no problem proving it to him if she had to. King had fallen for too many tricks concerning pregnancies and he really didn't need another woman pregnant right now. He would feel better if he saw a pregnancy test for himself.

"When did you find out? I mean wow! Wait…are you calling me because you think I'm the daddy?" King asked.

"King, don't make me come through this phone and slap you. I haven't had sex with any other man unprotected in a long, long time. You can take a paternity test if you want to. You know I don't play those types of games," Delishus said.

"Okay, yeah, I believe you and all. It's just weird timing. Give me about an hour and I'll be over there," he responded, rubbing his forehead. She agreed to be home when he finished meeting with Dino. "My life is steady snowballing man. Damn!" he said, hanging up the phone.

Dino wiped his mouth with a napkin. King watched him admire a woman's picture on his phone and assumed she was the woman he had mentioned earlier. "What's wrong?" Dino asked.

"Man, you do not want to know! My baby mother told me she was pregnant and now my side chick telling me she's pregnant. I don't know which one of them to believe! Feel like I'm in a damn twilight zone!"

"Trust me, I have been down that road before. That's what made me become a one-woman man. All that drama can kill a brotha," Dino advised drinking his beer.

"Yeah, I bet. You need to stop lusting over that picture and let's get back to business at hand," King said, attempting to rush their meeting.

"You're the one whose phone is blowing up," Dino laughed.

"Dude, this over here is way more than any man should have to deal with. I got too many bitches and it seems like the more I try to get my shit together, the more they interfere. Unlike you, I juggle women daily. But with you helping me at the gym, I can make that a thing of the past. I can't say that I have a woman that I love as much as you do. For now, love is on the back burner until I get myself together. I want to win a few title matches, get my own crib, and dump all these disloyal women for the kind of woman you mentioned earlier. I want a thick chick I can wake up to; one I wouldn't mind having kids with. The hood rat I got at home ain't worth it," King advised.

"Well, I like you King and as long as I know you're going to take this thing serious, I don't mind helping you out. I will have to charge a fee though," Dino advised.

"Okay, my shawty got the check, so we'll talk dollars once you show up for the first day of training. If you can get me into any matches, that's extra money or bonus. If I win a match, then I will pay you twenty percent of my earnings. Do we have a deal?" King asked, extending his hand.

Dino hesitated but then reached out, cracking a smile. "Deal... Oh and if I heard you correctly, you said you want a thick woman? Well, Tina has a few friends that come in from time to time. They may be just what you are looking for," Dino said, shaking King's hand back.

"They gotta weigh 200 pounds or more. If not, then I don't want them. I like my women BBW like Drake says in the song," King commented thinking about Delishus.

"Ain't nothing wrong with that my man. Nothing wrong with that at all," Dino said smiling back. That outing marked the beginning of a great friendship.

CHAPTER 12: A BBW TYPE OF LOVE

DELISHUS

Delishus went to the door after hearing a knock. When she saw Germane, she stood on the other side of the door contemplating if she should let him in. After opening the door, she realized she needed to see Germane to get some issues off of her chest. With King probably on his way, she needed her talk to be brief.

"What Germane?" she answered without a smile.

"Hey baby, what's wrong?" he asked.

"You! I could have sworn I told you not to contact me anymore. The way you acted the other night at the club pushed me away from you. And I think we should fall back from each other. I'm gonna do me and you can do you."

"I don't want to see other people though. I want to be with you, Delishus. I love you! Whatever I did the other night, I'm sorry! Please forgive me," Germane begged and dropped to his knees in the doorway.

Her eyes grew big, noticing that he was willing to plead his case. And not to mention that he also used the "L" word. She was confused but knowing that she was pregnant by King, there was no way she could be with Germane. She didn't want to hurt his feelings, so it was best to break things off before he found out she was pregnant by someone else.

"Germane, you are a nice guy boo, and there are plenty of other women out there. Hell, for all you know you could be missing your soul mate, waiting around for me to get serious with you. It may be hard for you to comprehend right now, but you will thank me later," she said trying to close the door.

"Wait a minute!" he said, pushing on the door and standing back up on his feet. His eyes were low and his heart got tight inside his chest.

"Goodbye Germane," she said, forcing it closed. He continued knocking and rather started beating on it like a crazed person.

"Let me in! I just want to talk to you, we can work this out!" Germane shouted, kicking the door.

"Are you crazy? Stop kicking my damn door! Go away before I call the police on you!" she yelled. He continued knocking and then a minute passed to where she didn't hear him. After a few minutes with no action, she figured Germane had given up and went on about his business. She walked into the bathroom and took a quick shower to clear her thoughts. Once she lay in the bed, she heard another knock at her front door. Picking up her cell phone, she entered 9-1-1 just in case she needed to call it. The behavior Germane showed her earlier proved he could be dangerous with his feelings for her. She figured they should have some space between them for the time being.

"Who is it?" she answered.

"King," he responded. She rushed to open the door, letting him in and checking behind him. She could tell that he came straight over to her house because she could smell the grilled food aroma coming from him.

"You expecting someone else?" he asked, waiting for her to close the door.

"No, not really. I was waiting up for you."

"Oh, well why are you looking out the door and stuff?" he asked, then he turned and looked behind himself as if someone was coming behind him.

"Nothing, some damn kids were playing on my door earlier and I thought you were them. Thanks for coming. I missed you," she said, hugging him tight.

"I missed you too. So are you for real about being pregnant by me?" he said, swallowing hard and looking her dead in her eyes.

"Yep, I have no reason to lie. I honestly wish I wasn't," she said, raising an eyebrow and releasing a deep sigh.

"Why not?" he asked, now offended by her gesture.

"Do I really have to answer that King? You already know the answer. It's because you live with your fiancé and have two kids by her. I wasn't trying to become just another baby momma," Delishus advised, lowering her head.

"Delishus, you would never be considered as just a baby momma. I told you that I loved you, and I meant that. What I have over there with Harmony is a done deal, if I can get a woman like you to be by my side. She doesn't like me boxing, but you love it. She isn't smart or sexy like you. I just don't want to leave her and then end up broken-hearted if you decide you want another man," King advised, lifting her chin so their eyes could meet.

"Being with you is all that makes me happy. But don't think for one minute that I will allow you to play house over here *and* over there! It's all or nothing with me."

"Well, what about your friend I saw you with the other day? You chose to spend time with him rather than with me," King pointed out.

"He was just a friend. And we don't talk anymore. Once I missed my period, I knew something was wrong. And I have no doubt that it's your baby. I wouldn't feel right putting off a child on a man who wasn't the real father. Not unless the father decided not to be in my child's life," she explained. "If you were my man, I wouldn't mind spoiling you and making sure your career was where you wanted it to be. But you would rather sleep with the dragon in the dungeon than to come live with me. I have the right to be concerned with your happiness, which I am. And you can't tell me that you're happy and that you're in love with that bitch, Harmony," Delishus said.

"Try not to worry about Harmony. She will be out of my hair in a little while. But for now, don't stress or think about any drama. As long as you want me, then we can be a team together. I take care of my kids. I wouldn't even want you to raise my child with any other man, having the child think that was a total stranger. I'm going to get on my feet and help you as much as I can. As a matter of fact, I just met with a trainer and coach whose going to assist me in getting where I need to be."

"Really? That's wonderful!" she said excitedly. She didn't doubt that King would be there for the child, regardless of them being together, but what Delishus was trying to avoid was having to deal with Harmony's ass altogether.

"Yes! I thought you would like the sound of that! So, for my first fight, I want to make sure I get you tickets to sit front row and center. Come out and root for your nigga," King said smiling. She couldn't help but feel butterflies as she laughed and kissed him.

"You know I will!" Delishus responded. They kissed and hugged for a few minutes, he really felt comfortable around her. He laid her down on the sofa and made love to her for the next hour and took a quick shower with her. Then King prepared to set off to get home before Harmony called him again. He hated when Delishus acted all sensitive, but her pretty brown eyes were what made King always come back to her. Looking in them, he saw nothing but a genuine heart. He hated breaking that motherfucker every other day. He hoped that one-day things would change financially, so that he could be with

Delishus, instead of Harmony. Feeling better about their talk, Delishus walked him to the door and turned off all the lights in the apartment. A couple minutes later, she heard a knock. Thinking that it was King, she opened the door smiling, then her smile faded when she saw that it wasn't him.

"Germane, I told you to go away," she said, getting more scared than nervous at his presence. His eyes looked red and he appeared to be a little jittery.

"I'm not leaving here until you tell me that you love me," he whispered. She could barely hear him.

"Goodnight," she said, closing the door. But this time, he had already stuck his foot in the doorway. She slammed his foot a couple times, attempting to get rid of him. He shoved the door open, forcing her back so hard she nearly lost her balance. He got inside, grabbed her by the wrist, covered her mouth with the other hand, and kicked the door closed with his foot. She felt his strength, but she didn't know what he'd done to her so quickly. Her heart was racing fast and she was nearly about to pass out from the pressure that he was applying on her mouth.

"Just be easy," he said in a low whisper. With King already on the way home, there was no one who could save her from him.

CHAPTER 13

"I'm sick of you treating me like I don't matter, like I'm a second hand bitch or something. Like I ain't hold yo' ass down while you was in prison. Bringing you loud and pills through visitation. Buying you cell phones every time you asked. Go here, go there. Nigga you got me fucked up! Maybe we should stop fuckin' around fa real fa real," Harmony was going off, yelling and rolling her neck all at the same time.

King looked up at her in his drunken state, barely able to comprehend what she was so upset about this time. Every now and then, they would argue about him being out late. This time King came home early, thinking he had done a good thing. Harmony went searching through his call log while he was asleep. Finding out that he was keeping secrets from her regarding having Delishus as his side chick, pissed her off to no end. She really thought that they reached a mutual understanding the last time they talked about getting married.

"What's the problem now?" he asked her.

"You! What am I to you? Is Delishus some late-night booty call, or whatever you consider her to be? If you're going to be coming up in here, then you need to help pay some bills. Try giving me some money for these lights to be on nigga!" she fussed.

"How am I goin' to pay bills that ain't even yours? Debra pays for the lights to be on up in here, not you! What you think I am, some trick or somethin'?" King replied, laughing in disbelief.

"Hell yeah!" she cursed back, proving she meant every word.

"Well, I ain't. You got me all the way fucked up! You're the reason why I was never able to save any money when I was hustling. You spent it all up as soon as I made it. What I got to buy you shit for when you got more money than me?" he told her, getting up to get dressed. He stumbled, hitting his knee on the cheap ass coffee table sitting in front of the couch. She giggled, noticing his level of intoxication.

"Thought you were out discussing business," Harmony stated, trying to change the subject.

"I was! I came home and drank from a bottle off the wet bar. Shit, that's what the liquor in the house is for, ain't it? Damn! You stay bitchin' and complain about something!"

"Whatever! Why are you texting and calling her still? I have a right to bitch this time seeing those messages from you to her. How could you lie to me after all we been through?" she said softly.

"I'm not the only one lying, I know that much," he responded. He wasn't about to fall for her sweet antics this time around.

"But you told me that you loved me. Don't you care about things I need in life? Like having a roof over my head, having utilities, or having food to eat?" Harmony said pouting.

"I do love you. What the hell trickin' got to do with love though? Hoe, we done been over this I don't know how many times. If you can't take this type of love I'm offering, then it is what it is. All these other women out here waiting to take yo' place will be glad when I tell them we ain't together no more. No man wants a woman at home to be bitchin' in his ear every day! When I go over there it's because I don't want to hear all this damn complaining about what I'm doin' wrong!" King shouted back, irritated from her disrupting his sleep. She grabbed his arm, preventing King from pulling up his pants.

"And no woman wants to have their family living with their mother. We are two grown ass people and should be able to do good on our own!" Harmony argued.

"Deciding to live here wasn't long term for me. You trippin' over nothing. We can move out into our own house right now. Why would I want to live in the house with my girl's mother? Everything I do is to get us into a better situation, but you're too stubborn to see it. I ain't the man I used to be in the streets and I don't wanna go back to being him," King advised.

"Wait! Okay...damn. King, I do appreciate you. I'm thankful for everything you do. But don't I deserve something in return from you other than sex and love? I want a big house with money in my bank to last me a long time. Wasting time and money on boxing isn't something I can agree that you should do. If you want to do it though, I can't do nothing but respect that. You would make more money out here hustling though," she said. King snatched away from her, letting her vent while he zipped up his pants and picked up his shirt off the floor.

"Harmony, my money from the streets could never be forever. You gotta think past that simple ass mind frame. You want a Trap King because you're so caught up with being a Trap Queen. That shit ain't me no more. Arguing about me cheating on you and wanting to box just proves that we are not compatible. How long have you known me? Being a freeloader isn't my thing, but that's what I feel like I've been reduced to. Of course, I will spoil you once I get my shit together, but for right now, you should be spending money on me to make our dreams a reality. And just so you know, this dick ain't free! You know I ain't got no job right now," King vented before putting on his shirt. He was thirty-eight, hot and didn't care what he said to her. She stood there quietly trying to collect her thoughts.

"I don't want you talking to Delishus!" Her hands went to her waist.

"Well she's in the same condition as you, so I can't stop talking to her," King confessed.

"What you mean same condition as me? You tryna tell me that she's pregnant? Is it your baby?" Harmony asked, getting pissed off.

King continued putting on his shoes noticing that he had them bitches on the wrong foot. He remained silent ,not wanting to dwell on the statement he had made. Harmony was far from done discussing the subject though. It never dawned on her that she would have to fight for King's heart like this.

"Fuck!" he cursed out loud taking the moment to sit down and swap shoes. "I'm not about to stop messing with her. Yes, she is pregnant by me. Shit happens!" he finally responded.

Harmony threw her shoe at him, hitting him in the back. "You motherfucker! No, shit doesn't just happen! How the hell you gonna get her pregnant? She better not think she is goin' to come before me and my kids! I can't believe yo' ass," she said with her voice trailing off. He knew tears would follow soon, so he rushed to get out of the house.

"I need some fresh air. I'll be back," he told her walking out the door. "Talking about a damn booty call. Don't tell me I need to start bringing out contracts for these hoes!" King mumbled to himself leaving her in the bedroom alone.

She heard the car engine purr and knew he was heading somewhere. If she didn't want to kill King's ass before, she damn sure wants to do it bad now. She really had no intentions of going through with Debra's plan, but she was all in now. An enormous amount of hate began to overcloud her love for him. Thinking about it, she might just have to hurry up with her plans to marry him so that Delishus couldn't reap the benefits of having her child with him. "Fuck nigga gonna make me put a price on his head", she said to herself with tears in her eyes.

*****

He parked his car and sighed heavily. Once he reached her door, he knew she would curse him out for showing up without calling. King knocked on Delishus' door, hoping he could sleep in her bed for the first time tonight.

"Can I help you?" Germane said, answering through the door.

"Uh yeah, I need to talk to Delishus," King said. He was surprised that Germane could be at her house this time of night and wondered if Delishus was actually playing him too.

"She's sleep. Who is it?" Germane asked, biting on his fingernail, peeping through the peephole and hoping he would leave.

"It's King. I was here a couple hours ago. Just tell her I'm outside and she will know what I need to talk to her about," he answered.

"This isn't a good time right now, brah," Germane said, trying to give King a good reason to leave. He didn't expect King to come back to her apartment after he witnessed him leaving earlier.

"Sho' nuff? Well, tell her to call me," he said not knowing what else to do. It was strange how she had poured her heart out to him only a short while ago and now she had a lame answering her door. "Guess she full of shit too! She obviously didn't expect me to return. Trying to play me, I'll show her ass too," he said, walking back to his car. He assumed Delishus was different and now felt that he was wrong about her too. He didn't know who the fuck to trust or believe. After cursing himself for getting caught up in this situation, he headed home and tried to return as neutral as possible, considering his idea of sleeping at Delishus' house flopped.

"Where you go to?" Harmony asked when he came back into the house. He laid down on the bed without responding to her. "Hello? You hear me talking to you King!" she said, interrupting his thoughts.

"What? What do you want from me Harmony?"

"I don't like how you just up and left the house. I want you to stop talking to her or else you will be out on the streets," she threatened without turning around to face him.

"Aight, say no more," he mumbled as if he gave a damn.

"I'm serious this time, King!"

"I said okay! Damn, a nigga bout to marry yo' ass, so stop whining and take yo' ass to sleep. My happiness with *money* is all that I care about. My heart will never stop loving that. Be glad I'm allowing you to be in my life, period," he responded.

"Are you sure you can just love me and forget about her? We can make our *own* money together," Harmony said, staring into his eyes once she turned to him.

"Yeah, I've been thinking and I feel we should get married in a few months. I can't just stop dealing with her because she is having my child. If you want to marry me, then you will have to understand and accept that. I don't want to hear no talk about her in a negative way again. We are all going to be a family soon," King advised.

He felt as if she was talking crazy now. There's no way he would leave Delishus alone. He still had love for her even after she pissed him off by having Germane over when he left. He couldn't even get mad after the many times he'd played her for Harmony. Delishus was a thick girl with a lot of meat on her, and he enjoyed that better than a petite woman such as Harmony. Harmony didn't have the looks, but she had big breasts and her ass was fat. She also had the one thing that King would always put first, and that was money! He peaked at his phone, seeing that Delishus still hadn't called.

"I got to get some sleep so I can work out in the morning. We'll talk some more about this at another time," he told her. King reached out to kiss her on the cheek before Harmony turned her face, rejecting his affection. Getting another woman pregnant would take some getting used to. As for right now, she still couldn't grasp the truth he spoke and wished he would find out Delishus was pregnant by someone else like she was.

"Don't try to kiss me, nigga. Go home to that ugly ass bitch you got waiting for yo' broke ass!" Harmony said, folding her arms across her chest. "Money won't mean anything when it's all gone because we wasted it on your stupid dream and that chunky bitch of yours!"

Before Harmony could utter another word, he reached out and slapped some sense into her. She lay there stunned, holding her face, remaining quiet. He could feel his nostrils flaring and was daring her to say another word at that moment. She allowed a tear to trickle down her cheek. Dissing King's career goals was no different from the slap that he gave her in the face. King turned over and resumed the task of trying to get some sleep. She might be cursing him out in silence, but he dared her to utter another word. If she didn't watch how she talked about Delishus, he wouldn't hesitate to lay hands on her again.

"Don't ever disrespect her again!" he said resting his eyes. King considered Harmony as his top bitch. His mental rolodex consisted of several women of his choosing, but none of them compared to Delishus. Contemplating the other women in his life, he thought about how he had his "bottom of the barrel" type as he liked to call them, which meant he only hit those females up when he was desperate for money or sex. No way could he call one of them up to rekindle any old flames. Then he had his average hoes that were only fucked with when his top bitches were slippin'. The way things were looking, both Harmony and Delishus were slipping. Harmony was not wife material, but she wanted to be married so badly. She didn't even take care of their kids and that was a must. So, as far as the eye could see, Delishus was right about him not being happy with Harmony. He didn't have any other woman to go to, so it looked like he was stuck. A few minutes passed before King finally drifted off to sleep after another stressful day.

Chapter 14

He was tired of women not taking him serious. For years, he had given his heart, money and time to women only for them to end up dumping him. *Not this time,* Germane thought. He entered the room, waking Delishus up by dashing ice-cold water on her. She screamed as she woke up realizing that she was bound and tied up to a chair. A glimpse around the room revealed that she was still in her apartment.

Well, at least someone will come looking for me, she said to herself. She screamed insults at Germane, even though he couldn't understand what she was saying.

"Huh? I can't hear you?" he said holding his hand behind his ear.

"Wait 'til I get out the damn chair, I'm going to fuck you up!" she cursed. Her words were unclear because of the tape that covered her mouth.

"Aw, do you have something to say?" he asked, leaning in to taunt her. She nodded her head and shook in the chair attempting to get loose. He removed the tape, gently letting her breath through her mouth.

"HELP! SOMEBODY HELP—" she screamed until Germane placed his hand on her mouth forcefully. She bit him on the hand ,finding a bone she hoped to do damage to. He screamed from the pain and struck her in the eye, causing her to let go of his hand. There was a shriek from her and some teeth marks on his hand once he took a look at it. He quickly covered her mouth back up with the tape.

"You fuckin' bite me! You bitch!" Germane said, trying to stop the bleeding. He raced out of the room to get a towel. He rinsed it off, clearing the blood so that he could see how bad she bit him. Delishus howled from the pain and cried from fear of not knowing what his motives were.

"I should have never let that motherfucker in my house!" she cursed to herself. She couldn't see the swelling but could feel her eye getting puffy. She had never dated an abusive man before. If Germane didn't mind hitting on her, who knows what else he would do to her.

"Delishus, we can do this the easy way or the hard way. Since you can't cooperate, I guess we will have to keep your mouth taped up for now. When you feel that you can be a good little girl, then I will remove the tape," he said, preparing to walk out of the room. She began murmuring louder and bouncing in the chair to get his attention.

He held on to the towel, applying pressure to his hand. "Do you think you can behave now?" he asked her.

She nodded her head and tried to calm down. She only wanted to ask him one question and it was killing her that she couldn't find the answer to it without him saying it aloud. He removed the tape, but this time he yanked it from her lips causing them to burn.

"Ouch!" she hollered. "Why are you doing this?" she asked, not wanting to miss her chance to ask the question. Her eyes were tearing up and she was scared for her life.

"Because I gave you one choice to make but instead you went in the opposite direction, disregarding me," he told her.

"What did I do? I'm so sorry! I promise I won't do it again," she pleaded.

"I told you to give me a chance to be with you. However, you chose to be with that other nigga. What do you see in him? Huh? I mean I don't get you women. You find a man who really likes you but you kick him to the curb for a man who can't see straight, let alone be honest with you about having other women," Germane explained.

"What do you mean, you women? Why are you worried about me when there are a million other females that would adore you?" Delishus asked while still in tears.

"Because I like you that's why. I love a thick ass woman similar to your kind. BBWs, I think that's what they call your type of woman. But for some reason you all don't seem to love me. I have dated about ten of you all and so far I keep getting the same results."

"Ten women? Where are they now? I'm afraid to ask what the results were," she interjected.

214

"No, trust me; you don't want to know what the results were. Let's just say that hopefully, you can survive unlike them," he responded.

"I'm confused, Germane. If you love big women, then why not treat us like we are queens instead of treating us like slaves. You can't keep me here forever, someone will find me and see what you are doing. I would hate for something bad to happen to you," she told him.

"Is that a threat? And I am not nearly as worried as you should be. It's only a matter of time before you give in and love me back. I know you love me; it's King who is blocking you from showing me your true feelings," Germane said, frowning at the mention of his name. The crazed look on his face and in his eyes proved to Delishus that she should be careful in what she said next.

"I do like you, Germane. I would probably love you if you give me the chance to do so freely. Let me go. I will do whatever you ask. We can work this out," she begged.

He smiled for a second then his eyes got colder than before. "Why don't you big women give me your heart just as I give you mine? What did I ever do to deserve being treated so coldly?" he asked.

"It's not you, Germane. I like you. Hell I, uh…I love you…" she said, looking into his eyes.

"Really?" he replied.

"Hell yeah, I love your ass!" she said. *This fool is going to kill me! Shit I will say anything to get free,* she thought. "Can you untie me now?"

He stepped forward, gripping one of the ropes. But then he hesitated and took a couple steps back. "Naw, last time I fell for that I almost let one get away. You think you slick, Delishus! You almost had me going for a second. I know the minute I let you free, you will try to run away like Candy did. But she saw that her plan failed. You have to prove to me that you won't do anything crazy. For right now, let's just leave you in here. I'm sure you will think of a way to prove your love. Maybe we can make a baby together," he said laughing. Before she could protest, Germane covered her mouth and continued on with his sinister laugh.

"This nigga has lost his mind!" she said to herself.

Without the strength to scream or yell, she just slumped in the chair with an aching back. *Please Lord, let someone find me*, she prayed. Delishus heard the front door close to her apartment and closed her eyes. Maybe when she woke up, this horrible dream she felt she was having would come to an end...

*****

It had been a couple of days since Toya had heard from Delishus and she was getting a feeling that something wasn't right. She called her phone multiple times and sent her a few text messages. Thinking that she was just busy with her modeling, Toya went to the agency Delishus held a previous contract with and walked inside.

"Hey, I am here looking for my friend Delishus Jones. Has she reported in for any sessions lately?" she asked the secretary.

"Dee is one of my favorite models. Unfortunately, her contract ended with us a couple weeks ago. We don't have any new contracts listed in our database for her, so no, she hasn't been here," the young lady answered.

"Oh wow, really? Okay, thank you. I didn't know that," Toya said, then she turned around and walked out the door just as fast as she got there. Delishus always had a modeling gig in the works. She wondered what Delishus was doing now to get extra money to keep up with her usual shopping and pampering. Regardless of that, she couldn't understand how she and Delishus were just out kicking it and now she couldn't reach her. She passed by a "Missing Persons" poster spotting a picture of a woman who weighed close to Delishus and herself. It was the picture of the man next to the missing woman's photograph that made Toya's heart drop to the pit of her stomach. Whoever the artist was had to be a professional because he had every mark and detail down to perfection.

"Last seen leaving with this male. He was wearing a black hoodie and blue jean pants. Height 5'9", the poster read. "Damn, he looks just like Germane. Now I really have got to get a hold of Delishus after seeing this," Toya said as she snatched the paper off the utility pole. She jumped in her car and headed to Delishus' brother's neck of the woods. She was driving like a mad woman, in and out of traffic, a side street here and left turn there. Fifteen minutes later, she was on the West side of Atlanta. She went to the door of the trap house where he hustled and knocked.

"Hey Toya, what's up?" he said, answering the door looking her in her eyes.

"Hey Tee," she said, and then went on. "I've been calling yo' sister and I think something has happened to her."

Tee raised his eyebrows. "Have you been to her crib?" he asked.

"Not yet," she said with a shaky voice. "I just think something is wrong."

Tee put his hand on her shoulder. "Calm down, I'll call around to see if somebody else has seen or heard from her," he said and pulled out his trap phone. "

CHAPTER 15

"I can't believe you letting that nigga live in the house after getting that bitch pregnant. Why you still fucking with King?" her friend, Savannah, asked.

"Don't worry about me! Bitch, worry about why yo' man don't come home at night. At least I know where King is all the time," Harmony argued. She flipped through the clothes on the rack in search of something that didn't show her stomach as much. It was taking time for her to adjust to being pregnant.

"But my man ain't never got another hoe pregnant. Talk all you want, but your sad ass in the same boat as me," Savannah responded, rolling her eyes.

"Yeah, just admit it Harmony, you sprung off that dick and King got you hypnotized. Ain't no way I could still be with his ass after everything he is putting you through," Tiffany chimed in.

"Whatever! If either one of you were in my shoes, you wouldn't know what to do until the situation actually happened to you. I know both of y'all love the hell out of your men so don't try to front. You would be trying to work things out too. Especially if he was your golden ticket to not having to work for the rest of your life," Harmony stated.

"What you mean by that? Tiffany asked.

"Yeah, King broke as hell! You can keep his golden ticket and trade that motherfucker in for three others that will be way more than his true value!" Savannah said, laughing and slapping five with Tiffany.

"Very funny, make fun of him all you want but when I cash in on this insurance policy, you bitches gonna have y'all hand out wanting some of my money. Speaking of which, if you keep on cracking jokes, I bet you I end up being the only one laughing walking out this damn store with merchandise," she warned. Tiffany and Savannah wiped the smiles off their faces, knowing that she wasn't kidding with them. Neither of them had a dime to their names and flocked to Harmony to help spend her money.

"We was only kidding bitch," Tiffany said, being the first to make sure Harmony didn't make her put the items she picked out back where she found them. Unbeknownst to them, Toya had entered the store in search of Delishus, but stopped once she heard a familiar voice. Standing behind the rack, she caught a glimpse of Harmony with her friends and paused at the mention of King's name.

"Uh huh. That's what I thought. Anyways, he doesn't have long to live and fuck around like he thinks he does," Harmony explained.

"We are not psychic so please elaborate on what the hell you are talking about!" Savannah said.

"There is no elaboration needed. Just what I said. King doesn't have long. His days are numbered. After we get married, I am going to make sure I sign the insurance papers as his wife. Then when it's time, his ass will be in the dirt, regretting that he ever broke my heart. It's one thing for a man to cheat on me, but to get a bitch pregnant in the process is just too much. Why do men even date fat broads? Like, what do they see in them?" Harmony rambled. Toya's eyes got buck after hearing what she thought she heard. She covered her mouth in shock. Could Delishus be pregnant by King? Now she really needed to find her friend and fast! She continued to listen, thinking that Harmony may know where Delishus was.

"I have tried to understand that too and I swear I can't understand why they do it. Well since you having his ass murked, then forget about him. And fuck that fat hoe he creeping with too. I hope you ain't planning on sharing none of the money with her," Tiffany stated.

"Hell nah I'm not! Why would you say some stupid stuff like that?" she said, frowning at her.

"I was just making sure. She is pregnant by him so isn't she entitled to some of his money to care for the child?" Tiffany responded.

"Nope, she can get it from the next nigga. She might be lying right next to King if they keep playing with me. I bet that's not even his baby," Harmony continued.

"Damn, I hope you two don't have the same due date. When is the baby due?" Savannah asked her. They walked up to the counter preparing to check out with Toya following, acting as if she was a customer checking out items in the store.

"I don't have but a few months left. As fat as she is, even if I saw her right now I probably wouldn't be able to tell how far along she was," Harmony joked. They burst into laughter placing their items on top the counter once it was there turn. Toya wanted to fight them all but knew she was outnumbered. She walked out of the store in search of King and Delishus, hoping to get some answers.

CHAPTER 16

His workout was going the way he wanted. After a few weeks of training, he was finally seeing results. His first big match would be coming up in another month and he couldn't wait to show everyone what he was made up.

"Aight, I'll see you tomorrow," King said waving goodbye to Dino. They had just left the gym and his new friend was dropping him off at home. He walked up to his porch, spotting Tori who was passing by him walking with an unfamiliar face.

"What's up, Tori?" he called out. Tori looked his way but turned his head without answering him. Tired of his attitude and feeling pumped up from the sparring session he just had, King decided to approach him.

"Yo' brah, Tori! I'm talking to you!" he said, getting within distance.

"Yeah, I hear you. What the fuck you want?" he responded back.

"I was just speaking but you got an attitude for nothing homie. You got a problem with me?" King asked. The guy Tori was walking with alternated glances between both men, not sure of the dilemma.

"Cuz, I ain't got time to deal with you. Yo' ass always want some attention. You must have me mistaken for one of yo' hoes. You need to find somebody else to kiss your ass. As far as I'm concerned you don't do shit, so you don't run shit no more. Got all these folks whispering in your ear like you the man," Tori said.

"Do I detect a hint of jealousy? Damn cuz, you don't have to be jealous of me. I appreciate you looking up to me and all, but to be the man you have to earn respect. A young nigga like you think you can just push a few pills and pounds, but it ain't that way in real life. This ain't TV, dawg. You have to really hustle and grind out here. You ain't grinding because you still nickel and diming bags! Step yo' game up before you try to clown me! We're supposed to be family, my nigga," King said to him.

"Well family is supposed to fuck with you. When was the last time you really fucked with yo' kind? Huh? You out here giving back to the community? I don't see King's name on anything out here. Get out my face with that bullshit," Tori said, taking a step in his face.

"Tori, we could really use another man to help with the job. Why not let yo' cuz in on the lick?" the other dude asked. Tori cut his eyes at him and returned to mugging King. He definitely had animosity towards him, mainly because Harmony had got all the way in his head. And it wasn't a better opportunity than now to finally get him out the way. Now with a change of heart, he finally said, "Pimp ain't ready for these type of jobs," his eyes were on Benzo, then he looked into King eyes for a moment.

"Well, we ain't got time to worry about that. Hey, I'm Benzo," the man said to King, holding out his hand for him to shake. Tori had met Benzo years ago when they were in Augusta Youth Development Center together and they remained in contact with one another. They did a few home invasion robberies together and caught a sweet lick on some Mexicans in Gwinett County for three hundred pounds of marijuana and seventy thousand dollars cash, however, that wasn't for King to know. Tori really didn't appreciate him putting King in his business, but since he'd had new plans for him, it didn't matter now.

"I'm King," he said and gave his hand. "What type of job y'all got lined up?"

Tori sighed, he was having mixed feelings now, really not wanting to bring King in on the jewelry store heist that they had planned. *Fuck*! he said to himself.

"We put together a plan to hit up the jewelry store. My girl work there and last week she had to work overtime. She saw how they closed up the store and opened it during her shifts. It's easy money, I'm talm' 'bout stupid sweet if we get in and out. I was telling Tori about it, but it's just us two and I think it would go a lot smoother with more manpower," Benzo explained.

"A jewelry store? Really? How much money they pull in?" King inquired, rubbing the hairs on his chin. He could use a little extra money for numerous of things, like getting himself his own spot to live in. And of course, if he mentioned it to Maliki, he might be all for helping out as well.

"Yeah, I think they bring in anywhere between twenty and fifty grand in the morning and at the close of the shift for bank drops. Of course, we plan on taking some merchandise but we have to choose wisely so that whatever we take doesn't get traced back to us. We wanted to hit up a few more places, but the jewelry store has the biggest bank," Benzo told him. King saw nothing but dollar signs and was even more eager to join now. He had two more mouths to feed and with a little money in his pocket, he could start saving for their futures. He tried not to, but he breezed through the money that he had saved at his Uncle Bo's house in no time. This could very well be the big break that he desperately needed.

"Fuck it, count me in. You sure there is no way we could get caught?" King asked.

"Only way we will get caught is if you fuck up," Tori chimed in laughing. King shot him a hard stare and ignored his comment.

"I got a buddy that can probably supply a whip or drive for us. Y'all got a getaway planned?" King asked, looking at them both.

"Naw, we hadn't quite got that far yet. If you or your friend can come up with something, let me know. Here, I'll give you my number, just in case," Benzo said. King took out his phone and entered in the digits as Benzo called them out.

Tori frowned at the thought of having to work with King, now he was trying to involve someone else. He already knew who he had in mind without even having to ask. "It's funny how you're so quick to include Maliki, but forget about the rest of us when it was time to get money," Tori commented bitterly.

"Maliki is my partna and he knows how to get shit done! Shouldn't be a big deal letting him in on the cut,

231

since he will be our key to getting home. What's the split going to be? Should be equal since it's equal participation," King said.

"Damn lie! Equal my ass! I'm the one who suggested we rob them. Benzo is the one with all the details and who discovered the good money making opportunity, so we get more of the split than you two!" Tori stated.

"Tori, come on. They in on the lick and if his man can get us out of there without getting caught then they deserve a fair share. Me and Tori were splitting 60/40 at first. We will still split that way and let you and your friend split the forty percent while we split the sixty, Deal?" Benzo interjected. He reached out his hand once again to seal the deal with King. Before Tori could protest, their hands met and concluded the meet.

"Bet!" King said, leaving them as they were before he walked up. He hurried to dial Maliki and went into the house. It didn't matter if Tori wanted him to join in or not. Benzo said he could so now all he needed to do was bring Maliki up to speed. They would work out the plans of the heist at a later time. But for now, business had to be discussed with Maliki.

*****

King met up with Maliki so they could discuss some things in private. While he was at Maliki's house, his uncle Bo stopped by as well. "Are you sure you want to go in on this deal with Tori? He's my son and all, but I consider you as a son too, King. I wouldn't be able to live with myself if something were to happen to you," Bo advised him.

"Unc, I'm cool! I appreciate your concern, but I gotta get this check, a nigga out here hurtin'. Harmony pregnant and I got another baby on the way by this chick named Delishus. With those two mouths, plus the two I already got, this offer is just too good to pass up. Besides, Benzo and Tori said that it's a solid plan," King said.

"I know. Be careful, alright? There are some things about Tori that you do not know," Bo stated.

"Well if you say I'm yo' son, then quit all that beating around the bush. Tell me what the deal is," King said.

Maliki swallowed hard because he already knew the information. Bo and him were holding back on. Giving the history of Tori and King, there were times were they hated each other. Bo felt it was best if he stayed out of their feud, so that it wouldn't turn into anything worse. However, after hearing that they were about to do a job together, Bo decided to tell King what he needed to know.

"I already told you I heard Harmony and Debra chatting the other day. What I didn't mention was that the baby that she's carrying is not really yours, King," Bo confessed.

King paused and let out a half laugh that didn't last long at all. "Come on Unc, you got to be joking right? How do you know?" His eyes were fixed on Bo.

"Because I heard it straight from the horse's mouth. Debra's mouth that is. Harmony admitted that it was by another man," Bo said, avoiding eye contact with King.

234

Maliki's eyes got bigger once he realized what Bo was explaining.

"I'ma kill that bitch! You tryin' to tell me that she got pregnant by another nigga and is trying to put it off on me?" King asked. "I knew that something wasn't right."

"Yeah, I hate to be the bearer of bad news. So, don't marry her King. She just wants to use you. Remember I told you they were plotting to use you as a pawn for an insurance deal," Bo advised him.

"Those two are trying to off my boy here?" Maliki asked, getting upset. King never mentioned this to him and he was worried that at any moment Harmony or Debra could proceed with killing King.

"Unfortunately yes, I overheard them talking," Bo answered.

"Well who the fuck she pregnant by then?" King asked. That's the question Bo feared to answer the most. He nodded his head and curled up his lip, not really ready to inform King of the truth. "I'm waiting," King said staring at his uncle. He got more and more upset knowing that he withheld this information all this time.

"I would rather not say," Bo replied, and it was hurting him dearly.

"Man, you did all this snitchin', you may as well go ahead and tell us. Don't let my guy find out later on that she's pregnant by some crazed maniac after he shoots up his spot looking for his kid," Maliki said.

"Tori," Bo just blurted out. "Your cousin is the name of the person I heard Harmony say she was pregnant by," Bo finally said, this time staring King in the eyes, letting him know he was telling the truth.

Maliki and Bo could see the look on King's face. The look of disgust, madness, and hurt all in one. They didn't know his reaction, but Bo was prepared for whatever to happen. "Sorry I didn't tell you. Harmony walked outside when I was about to," Bo told him, feeling remorseful. King couldn't even be mad at Bo because it wasn't his fault that his son took on a whole other level of being disloyal.

"Don't even apologize for their behavior Unc. Both of them are grown and made the decision to be together behind my back. I can't be mad at no one but myself for not seeing it coming. Tori has been giving me a crazy look since I got out. At least now, I know why. It's cool. Karma will come back to bite him in the ass for betraying me the way he did. But for right now, I got to get this money and I will do this job with him regardless of what you just told me," King advised Bo.

"Well like I said, just be careful. Watch your back around him and I will always love you, no matter what happens in the future. Don't let them win though. I always raised you to be a fighter. I want you to come out on top," Bo told him and started patting him on the shoulder. King hugged him and watched him exit Maliki's house.

"Damn, you took that better than I thought. Are you really still going to go through with this plan?" Maliki asked.

"You bet yo' ass. But instead of how they got it planned, you better believe I'm about to shake some shit up. Tori fucked over the wrong nigga. I got somethin' for his ass," King stated.

"I understand if you are upset. I have to apologize as well for not saying something to you when I saw her come from over his house. She never saw me but I always wondered what she was doing over there. I'm sorry man. Didn't think she was fucking dude though. So what you wanna do? Anytime I see a look like that on your face, I know you got something on your mind," Maliki commented.

"I think we deserve a bigger cut, don't you?" King asked. His eyes were serious and unreadable.

Maliki nodded his head. "Fuckin' right."

"Well let's pull this shit off like we use to back in the day. How does fifty-fifty sound?" King responded.

"Sounds like a plan to me," Maliki said. They sat down, putting their heads together. King let people blind him with far too many lies. It was now time for him to be the man that he used to be. No matter what his enemy had in the works, he was determined to defeat them. He wanted to win a title inside and outside of the boxing ring, now more than ever!

CHAPTER 17: FREE ME

DELISHUS

Toya banged on the door, hoping to knock it down. She heard no sounds coming from the inside. Delishus could hear the banging but wasn't able to get up from the chair. Still strapped to it for days, she began to smell sour. When no one came to the door, Toya left and headed straight for the police department. She filled out a missing persons report and made sure her details were similar to that of the missing persons report concerning the woman named "Candy."

Delishus couldn't get near her phone that was on the dresser. She saw it light up every time someone called and wished she could answer it. Luckily, it had stayed plugged in. Not knowing the time that she had been locked away, her stomach growled once she realized the small amounts of food Germane had been feeding her were not enough. Every day she thought she was getting closer to freedom only to find out that Germane had no intentions of letting her go. She heard him enter the apartment whistling.

"Hey beautiful," he said, smiling and kissing her on the cheek. She turned her head in disgust and frowned at his presence. She'd rather be there alone than to be with him. He removed the tape from her mouth as he did every evening when he came by to check on her.

"Whoa! Is that you smelling like that? We need to get you cleaned up," he said, untying Delishus one hand at a time. She was so weak from not eating that she could barely move.

"Germane, I need to eat... the little portions of food you give me are not enough..." Delishus whispered.

"I thought you liked Subway. I noticed you there one day and figured why not feed you what you like. Candy never liked anything I bought her. Don't turn into an ungrateful bitch now," he told her.

"I'm not being ungrateful. Candy couldn't have been a woman of my stature. I need more than just one 6-inch sub sandwich a day. Who do you think you are feeding?" Delishus responded.

"We can get you some fruits and vegetables next time. But look what I brought you," he said removing a shopping bag. He removed a blue dress looking to be in her size. The odd stains on it showed Delishus that it had been worn before though.

"A dress? I don't want a fucking dress, nigga, I need food! What the fuck is wrong with you?" Delishus said angrily. His expression made her quickly change her tone.

"Excuse me?" he said, holding up the dress for her to see it. "You don't like it?"

"I like it, it's just that I am really hungry Germane ,and if I don't eat something my baby could die," she told him.

"Baby? Who got a baby? You pregnant?" Germane asked. Forgetting that she hadn't broken the news to him, she quickly wished she could take her statement back.

"Um, yes I am... So you need to make sure I eat properly every day," Delishus responded.

"Oh yes! I have always wanted a baby. We can name him after my father if it's a boy. But I would really love it if you had a girl!" he spoke excitedly.

I know this fool doesn't think I am pregnant by him, Delishus said to herself. "Well I haven't exactly thought of any baby names but we will see. There will not be a baby if I can't get what I need. Germane, you cannot keep me trapped in here all day. I have to get up and move around some," Delishus said, getting a clear sight of the living room. Her mind toggled between ideas on how she could escape his crazy ass.

"Why didn't you tell me this sooner? Sorry that I hit you. No mother of my child will want for anything. Let me run your bath water and then I will go to the grocery store to get you some foods to eat."

"Thank you, can I go with you?" Delishus asked with a smile.

"Silly woman. No, I said I will go to the store. Tell me the things you need and I will get them," Germane said, turning on the shower water. He tested the temperature after guiding Delishus into the bathroom. He helped her undress and closed the door decreasing her chances of getting out. Once she got into the shower, he joined her and lathered up her bath sponge.

"Here, let me help you," he said, taking the time to bathe her body. She stood in the shower, wanting to drown him underneath the waters but didn't want to lose his trust. He smiled when cleaning her butt and washing her vagina. Once he got to her breasts, he massaged them and even teased her nipples. For some reason Delishus still managed to be turned on by his affection. He rinsed her body and dried her off. She thought he was heading into the living room, but instead he closed the bedroom door and forced her to lie on the bed. After getting her where he wanted her, he planted kisses on her body and licked on various parts of her body. She hated him for making her feel so good, but she didn't want him to stop.

"Can I have a taste? I want you so bad," Germane told her while whispering and blowing on her. She couldn't help her juices as they flowed when he stuck his tongue and finger inside of her simultaneously. "Mmmm, you taste so good," he stated.

She released a much-needed orgasm minutes later and felt the pressure once he forced himself inside of her. She placed her hands on him pushing him off but he only got more aggressive and dug deeper. She moaned and cried at the same time, wanting this nightmare to end. The sex he gave her was good, yet she didn't want it to be.

"Please stop," Delishus whispered. Germane turned her on her side and found her anal hole. He disregarded her request and pounded her without any lubrication or anything to help ease the pain. Delishus cried and hollered. Germane pumped slower, making sure she felt him and covered her face with a pillow. She fought to stay alive, but wished she were dead. The pain was excruciating and she felt violated in every way. This wasn't any ordinary sex. Delishus was raped and there was no one around to save her. Her eyes rolled into the back of her head and she gave up fighting and let him finish what he started. He released his semen in her and tied her to the bed. Delishus lay there shivering without any clothes on. *Where was her King when she needed him most*, she thought?

CHAPTER 18: My Time To Shine
KING

Within the next forty-eight hours, King was the first person inside the jewelry store with an Afro wig and a Braves fitted cap. Benzo followed in behind him, wearing women's makeup to hide their faces from the cameras.

"Nobody move!" King yelled, firing a single shot into the ceiling. Screams of fear came from the few people that were inside.

"You get over here!" Benzo ordered the jewelry store manager. The short Chinese woman trembled in fear, scared that today would be the day she lost her life if she didn't cooperate. Benzo grabbed her by the arm and roughly shoved her towards the cash register. "Open it right now…slowly though!"

King watched the door, making sure no one entered while they pulled off their fourth robbery in the last two days. They also hit up a post office, a local bank, and an armored truck that was leaving a mega church parking lot. King wouldn't stop until he did his final job.

Damn shawty you pretty and thick. Benzo said to himself, watching her with an evil eye, and King was watching him, the way he was looking at her. Then he said, "Nigga, are you serious? Hurry up and get the money so we can move! Stop all that eyeball rape shit," King demanded. He rotated his gun, shifting it from being pointed at each of the store customers and employees. The manager handed the money from the cash register to Benzo. He grabbed a few pieces of jewelry from behind the glass. He smashed one counter after another, making sure they were rewarded from this job. King and Benzo raced out of the back door to the store heading down the alley. Sirens could be heard in the distance proving that the police had been alerted of the robbery.

"Man, that was close! We did it!" Benzo said proudly and nearly out of breathe.

"Nah, we didn't do it, I did it," King said, and without warning, he raised his gun and aimed it at Benzo's head, putting a bullet right in the center of his forehead. It happened so fast that he didn't even see it coming. King snatched the loaded duffel bag from Benzo's hand, leaving his lifeless body in the alley. He dropped a couple pieces of hot jewelry on him so that when homicide did their investigation they would know he was part of the robbery. King then took the other street as planned. He knew to meet up with Maliki on the opposite end of the neighborhood. King ended up back on a main street, resulting in one police car gaining on his tail until he hopped a chain fence, landing into a backyard where there were two huge headed Rottweiler. King was fast and in shape, the dogs chased behind him until he hopped the fence just before they could get him. When he landed on the other side, he heard Maliki "Yo', over here!" King leaped over another wooded gate and tried to control his breathing. He peeked around the dumpster, spotting several police cars speeding past them.

"Damn, that was close," King said, resting against the dumpster. "How much cash did we score?" he asked. Maliki opened the sack and shuffled the bills around.

"I don't know, maybe a couple hundred," Maliki responded. Once the sirens subsided, King and Maliki stood up to head to their getaway car.

"Cool. Once we get to the crib, we can count that shit.

And split it up," King said in the calmest tone of voice, still trying to remain cool after dropping Benzo. No more than ten minutes later, they pulled up to a hide out spot where Tori was parked and waiting for them in another car. When they both stepped out and got in with Tori, the first thing he asked was.

"Where is Benzo?" Maliki ignored him and jumped into the Bronco.

"Man, we told him to keep up but I guess he got lost back there." King said to Tori.

"Yeah, he don't normally do no shit like that. Aight, where my cut at?" Tori asked.

"Right here…" King said holding up the gun to his head. Tori smirked and shook his head.

Tori frowned. "On know what you got on yo' mind, pimp, but you better get that gun out my face! I want my money! You better tell yo' man to chill!" Tori responded, looking at Maliki.

"He ain't got nothing to do with this, we on some personal shit now." King said, and by the look in his eyes, he was definitely serious. "Now, what's the business between you and Harmony? That's yo' bitch?"

"Yeah, so what? You gon' kill me 'bout a bitch? You don't deserve her and you out here chasing other bitches anyway! Fuck all that, where my dough at?" Tori asked once more. King smiled, shook his head side to side as he couldn't believe what he was hearing. Then his uncle Bob flashed in his head clear as day. King felt in his heart that Tori wanted to kill him and he definitely would if the shoe was on the other foot. He was too far to turn back now. Then he said. "I'll take care of your child for you." Then without warning, he pulled the trigger twice without any signs of emotions.

"Fuck you, nigga! You don't get no money from me!" King said, putting the gun in his pants. He took a few more pieces of the jewelry from the bag and scattered them beside Tori. He could never let anyone get over on him, not even family. Next, he planned to deal with Debra and Harmony. They hopped out of the truck and walked to

Maliki's car that was parked two streets over. Once they made it home safely, they were both able to breathe a little easier. King unlocked the door to Maliki's apartment with him following closely behind. The two counted the money and separated the jewelry. Maliki and King had been homies since high school and King never had to worry about Maliki doing anything foul to him. Damn shame he had to kill his own cousin because he couldn't trust him.

They would often pull off jobs together and sometimes had a crew of at least three other men to accompany them. Two of their homeboys were locked up for other reasons right now though. King didn't have parents to keep him out of trouble and looked up to Maliki as they got older. He taught King how to get money in the streets and how to survive the real world. After they cleaned up, changed clothes and got rid of the hot weapons, they were ready to celebrate. Next stop, Diamonds Of Atlanta.

*****

King entered the building with Maliki following. They counted out their money, making sure they had

252

enough ones to throw and enough to pop a couple bottles for the night.

"Hey baby, what's up? How 'bout a lap dance for my boy?" Maliki asked one of the familiar dancers. He flashed some money in her face, showing her that he was serious.

"Damn, you got ya weight tonight. Where yo broke ass get that money from? I know you ain't really rolling like that?" the stripper Jodi asked. She'd known King and Maliki to come into the strip club every other weekend. They really didn't stay long because their money wasn't long enough to make it even sprinkle, let alone make it rain.

"Don't worry about all that, me and my nigga pulled off a good lick," Maliki bragged.

"Aye man, chill with all that rapping. You know these bitches be talkin' and shit." King looked at the the chick Jodi. "Don't pay attention to him sweetheart, we made this money from doing a legit job, that's all that matters. Now come show daddy what you workin' wit," King stated.

"King? Is that you?" he heard a voice say behind him.

"Yeah, it's me." He turned around spotting a thick woman who looked familiar. She had a hand full of cash and rings on her fingers that glistened with diamonds even in the dark club.

"Hey, what up shawty?" he asked getting up to approach one of the waitresses. "How you been?" he said, hugging her until he noticed a familiar face across the club. *I'll be damned*, he said to himself. Germane was sitting directly across from them talking to another woman.

"Good. You want anything to drink?" she offered.

"Yeah, get me my usual. Say, do you know that dude over there sitting by the bar?" King asked, pointing in Germane's direction. She looked around at him.

"Oh Lord yes! The owner has put him out several times for being disrespectful to some of the dancers."

"Sho' nuff? I've never seen him here before so I was just curious."

"Yeah, that guy is a real piece of work. He comes off nice but then once you get to know him he is not so great. One of the dancers used to be his girlfriend a year ago. She disappeared for six months after meeting him. We haven't seen her since. Guess he must have ran her off because he would come in here every time her shift started. Whenever she would dance for our customers, he started fights with her and even pulled her out of here a couple of times. The manager figured she went to another club considering we hadn't seen her in a while. Until about a couple weeks ago, we hadn't seen him either," Jodi explained.

"Oh for real… that's crazy. I don't know if I would even want to date a stripper because I already know what comes with that lifestyle. So you say you haven't seen him in a while, huh? He got any new stripper girlfriends up in here?"

She laughed and shook her head. "Don't know if he is talking to any females in here again, but after the disappearance of Candy, nobody else would talk to him. He's got this creepy vibe to him. I'll be right back with yo' drink."

She walked off, leaving King to marinate in his thoughts. It had been days since he saw Delishus and he was really missing her. He wished he had her best friend's number, but he didn't know much about her. Just then, a thought hit him and he decided to act on it just to see where it would lead. He pulled out his phone and pulled up his Facebook account. After putting in Toya's name, he sent her a friend request right before he messaged her.

HAVE YOU SEEN OR TALKED TO DELISHUS? He typed. Thankfully, she was online at the time because she responded to him quickly.

NO, I GOT A MESSAGE SAYING SHE WAS GOING OUT OF TOWN BUT NO DETAILS OR EVEN

A CALL TO BRAG ABOUT WHERE SHE IS…THAT'S NOT LIKE HER AT ALL, Toya responded.

King didn't bother typing back. He didn't want to set off any false alarms. He logged off his Facebook account and smiled when Jodie brought his drink. Maliki was too busy watching two strippers dance and by the amount of fun he was having, King didn't want to interfere at the moment.

"Jodie, do you know if he has a thing for big girls?" King asked her before she walked away.

"Of course he does! Candy was a thick woman and she was one of our best big girl strippers, real pretty. He flirts with a lot of women no matter the size though. Seems like an all-around freak to me," she replied. That statement made him wonder what kind of man Germane really was. He needed to find out because it was bothering him that he could be in Delishus' house one day and now no one had heard from her. If he did something to harm her, King wouldn't hesitate to add him on the list of his most recent murder victims.

CHAPTER 19: RESCUE ME
KING

King looked down at his phone and wondered what Toya wanted with him. He quickly opened a direct message from her when he saw that the headline read "PLEASE CALL ME".

Dialing the number, he could see the message was only a few hours old. "Hello?" she answered. He could hear the panic all in her voice.

"Hey, this is King. I saw your message on Facebook, you wanted me to call you?" he said.

"Oh my God! Yes! You still haven't seen or heard from Delishus? I'm scared! I still can't reach her!" Toya shouted. He sat up in his seat, noticing her alarming tone.

"Mane, I've been calling and even went by the house to talk to her but she hasn't returned my calls. What's wrong?" he asked.

"I have a weird feeling that something is not right! Is she pregnant?" Toya responded.

"From what she tells me, yeah she's expecting. I went by her house the other day and she confessed that I got her pregnant," King said, holding his head down.

"Damn! I told you to lose her number when I should have been saying that to Germane instead. Have you seen him or do you know who he is?" Toya asked.

"Yeah, I saw him at her apartment some days ago. Why is she talking to him when she swears the baby is mine?"

"King, you have to find him! Germane is not who you think he is! I saw a mugshot drawn up on a sign! I believe he is responsible for kidnapping this woman named Candy. I took the poster—"

"Wait a minute. Did you say Candy?" he asked, jumping up from his seat fully alert.

"Yes! She was reported missing a while ago. I'm scared because they say she has been missing for months now. I've never seen the woman before but she looks heavy set like me and Delishus. Germane may have a thing for full-figured women and this could be another one of his kidnappings, if he is indeed the man from the picture!" Toya said in tears.

"Damn!" King said, shaking his head. He snatched up his keys from the counter and raced to the car.

"What?" Toya asked desperate for answers.

"That name sounds familiar. I was at DOA club the other night and a waitress pointed out Germane, saying that he was dating a stripper named Candy that worked there. They haven't seen her and if I remember, he was talking to a couple women that were on the plus size while I was there. I should have known something was wrong when I stopped by her house. I'm going back over there to see if he is still there. I mean he answered the door and everything like he lived there." King said.

"Please help me find her, King. I don't want anything to happen to my best friend! She actually loves you and I can bet you Germane is behind this. He flipped out one night when we went out dancing at a club. He came in, dragging her out and telling her to go home," Toya advised him.

"Don't worry. I'll lock your number in and call you the minute I have something," he told her.

******

He could tell something wasn't right with Germane from the time he saw him. If he picks up women in the strip club as often as the waitress advised, then something was wrong. The last time he saw him at Delishus' apartment he got a weird vibe but played it off. This time he was making it his mission to follow Germane.

"Hey Maliki, I need you to ride with me somewhere real quick," he told him. Maliki was so drunk that he just nodded his head and got up to follow behind him. He relaxed into the seat while King drove back to the club. As soon as they pulled up, King spotted Germane coming out of the club. His timing was perfect as King watched him get into his car and pull off.

King kept his distance to make sure Germane wouldn't see him trailing him. He watched him stop at a gas station for a pack of cigarettes. He had no clue where Germane lived or what he did for a living but every time he saw him, he was dressed like a damn professor or a preacher, wearing a nice suit and tie. King got an uneasy feeling just knowing that there was always a serial killer or rapist popping up every other year in Atlanta. And in all honesty, he'd been in prison with a few of them. Once he finally realized that Germane was heading back to Delishus' apartment, King felt his stomach turn flips.

"The nerve of this nigga. He ain't no different than me. I'll just have to make her ass see it! I can't wait to expose his ass." King got out of the car, noticing that Germane opened Delishus' door with a key. "So she giving him access to her house too? He could have easily brought a female in and had sex with her or let a stripper from the club dance for him," King mumbled to himself.

He looked over at Maliki who was snoring, and just shook his head. Before he walked over to the apartment, he turned down the music and tapped him on the shoulder. "Aye mane, I'm about to go check on shawty crib, I'll be right back." Maliki raised one eyelid and nodded his head before leaning forward.

"Ughhhh, I feel sick," he mumbled, placing his head in his lap while covering his face.

"Shawty, don't throw up in my damn car! I ain't tryna hear Harmony's mouth about cleaning it up. Stand up for a second. Get out of the car and get some fresh air," he suggested. When he didn't see Maliki do as he told him, he grunted and walked over to open the passenger door. "Come on, stand up man. I swear to God if you throw up in here, you'll be paying me $30 to get it shampooed and cleaned out."

"Alriiiight... damn," Maliki slurred. He stepped out of the car, leaving King with a sense of comfort knowing that he had Maliki catch a breather. King left his boy standing near the car as he walked up to Delishus' apartment. He tapped on the door but when he didn't hear anything, he got concerned. "Now I know I saw him go in here," he mumbled.

"Don't you make a sound!" Germane told Delishus as he put the tape back over her mouth. He had just finished running piping hot water and planned to wash her body up, considering that she had been tied to a chair for four days now. She wiggled and shook her head while trying to get free. He held a finger up to his lips after hearing someone at the door. "You expecting someone?" Germane asked, getting upset. I better not find out you've been naughty while I stepped out."

"This nigga is fuckin' NUTS! How the hell can I get free with all this tape and rope on me? If I got out, he better believe I would have left this apartment with the quickness and had his ass locked up for kidnapping!"

Delishus said to herself. She didn't know who was at the door, but she prayed that it was someone looking for her.

Germane looked through the peephole and tried to see who was at the door. He could tell that it wasn't a woman just by the way the person was knocking. It was nothing like the knock he heard the other day when Toya came by in search of Delishus. "Dammit! Why is he here?" Germane said, spotting King outside. "Who is it?" He straightened up his tie and cracked the door open with its chain still intact.

"Open the door, I want to talk to Delishus!" King answered. The baritone in his voice reached the bedroom causing her to get excited and yet fearful at the same time.

"Delishus isn't available right now. I'll tell her that you stopped by," Germane answered, preparing to close the door again. King observed the television off in the living room as well as most of the lights in the front of the apartment. The place looked gloomy like no one was home.

"I don't care what she's doing. Step aside and let me in. I want to hear her say that!" King growled.

Germane could tell he wasn't taking no for an answer so he closed the door and grabbed a wooden baseball bat that he had behind the door. Once he opened it, King walked inside looking around. He took at least four steps and was about to call out her name when Germane swung the bat and caught him across the back of his neck and head. The impact of the hit made him see stars immediately. His knees buckled underneath him and then everything went black.

When King came too, he found himself in a chair beside Delishus, duct taped and bound by rope. He could feel the blood seeping from the wound he suffered on account of the bat causing a gash. His head was hurting like hell and he was nearly out of it. Delishus cried and tried to talk once she saw that he was awake. He could understand her mumble of "I'm sorry" and put two and two together.

"It's okay. Are you alright? Did he hurt you?" he asked

her. Germane didn't have his mouth taped because he

assumed he would be knocked out cold for a while.

Inside the car, Maliki began to think, shaking himself out of his drunken mind state, now realizing that King should have came out by now. I know this nigga ain't leave me in no car while he went to fuck. He said to himself. He stepped out of the car to go get the keys and walked over to the apartment that he saw King go inside of.

Back inside the apartment, Germaine said. "Well, well,

well, glad to see that you have finally woke up. You two look good tied up together. Are you happy now? See what you made me do?" Germane said staring at both of them,

his eyes going from one to the other. But he stared hard at King, watching him bleed, watching him sweat, the anger and pain that was in his eyes told him that if he had the opportunity that he'd kill him.

"The minute I get free I'm gonna beat the brakes off yo'

ass. I put that on my kids, pimp!" King threatened.

Germane laughed, came out with a sharp kitchen knife and plunged it in King shoulder so fast that he didn't see it coming. "Beat the brakes off that." He said calmly and removed it, more blood begins to soak the front of his shirt.

"Aghhhh!" King screamed from the pain. Delishus hollered as loud as she could from seeing the horrific scene. Germane wiped the blood from the knife and put it close to Delishus cheek.

"That is what happens when you talk back thinking you're in charge. But you don't run nothing, I do! When I get through with you, King, I will dump yo' motha' fuckin' body in the Chattahoochee River and make sure it doesn't float to the top," Germane warned in the coldest tone of voice that he could pull up. Before he could speak, they all heard a knock at the door. "Oh my God! What's the deal with this place? Everyone wants to drop by, huh? Well it better not be your friend Toya again or else I am going to make her wish she was never a friend of yours at all!" A disgruntled Germane said stomping out of the room with the knife in his hand, drops of blood was falling to the carpet as he went.

Delishus looked at King as his eyes rolled to the back of his head. She called for him, attempting to keep him awake but it was no use. He still couldn't keep himself conscious with the severe wound that he suffered. Nor could he make out what she was saying with her mouth-taped shut. Having never seen Maliki before, Germane didn't know who he was. He opened the door assuming he was a neighbor or something.

"Yes, can I help you?" Germane said nicely while opening the apartment door. He held the knife behind his back, offering a crooked smile. Even in his drunken state Malaki noticed that the apartment looked awkward with all the lights off. Especially since he saw King go inside only a few minutes ago.

"Aye, what's good, brah? I'm looking for my potna'," Maliki stated. Once he heard Maliki's voice, King fought for his life and yelled out his name.

"Maliki! In here brah! Dude is bananas!" King shouted.

Maliki quickly sobered up enough to dodge Germane's

swift swing of the knife. He snatched his pistol from his waist, took a couple steps backwards and took aim with his Glock 40 and shot him in the chest twice. *Baka baka* the gun roared. Germaine stumbled backwards and fell in the middle of the floor. Delishus' muffled screams roared throughout the apartment, but King knew he had a chance to live once the shots were fired. Once Germane's body hit the floor, Maliki rushed through the apartment and raced to the back bedroom, seeing Delishus and King detained.

"What kind of freak shit y'all got goin' on in here?" he asked.

"Maliki," King said in a weak tone of voice, he said loosing a lot of blood now and his eyes were weak, nearly closed. "That nigga done lost his mind, shawty. Hurry up and untie me! Give me yo gun." He was ready to go straighten his face. He had to.

"You don't need no gun, brah, I handled that already. Damn! You pouring blood." Maliki fussed finally releasing King. He put his gun back in the waistline of his jeans and helped untie Delishus.

"Help me." King said and stumbled.

271

"Aw shit, brah let's get the fuck out of here. We don't need the cops coming in thinking you did anything since you're still on parole!" Maliki suggested. They helped Delishus up from the chair and were disturbed to find that Germane was no longer laying on the floor where he'd just left him.

"Where did that nigga go? I know I shot his ass!" Maliki stated. "I even seen him hit the floor."

"Did you shoot him in the head?" King asked, holding his shoulder.

"Damn, naw I didn't, you see him?" he asked, looking around the living room.

"No fool, because he's gone! Look at the blood trail leading out the door! You let him get away. He must've had on a vest." King said, slouching over.

Delishus looked at King and she immediately began to worry. "Oh my God! We have to get him to a hospital! Germane stabbed him!" Delishus said to Maliki while going over to help aid King. They walked him to the door and still saw no signs of Germane. His car was gone too, so there was no telling where he went. They fled the scene and headed straight to the hospital.

Chapter 20 My BBW and my Fiancée

King

Delishus slept in the hospital chair at Grady Memorial peacefully. She woke up every now and then, wondering where she was. He would assure her that she was in good hands and make sure she fell back to sleep. Even though she'd brought King to the hospital, she had had herself checked out as well. She was kinda disturbed by the situation and had definitely reported the rape. The doctors did a thorough examination on her to make sure that all was well. Her unborn baby was alright and that was all that she was worried about.

"How you feel, mama?" King asked her. His voice was soft and low, he'd been stitched up and put back together. However, his concern was only for her.

"I feel fine, but how are you? Are you okay?" she asked noticing, that he was finally awake. It seemed like whenever he dozed off from the medication, Delishus woke up. And when she was asleep, he was wide-awake contemplating his next move.

"Yeah, any idea where you can go until we can find you a new spot?" he asked.

"I have a few places that I can go. The thing is, do I wanna go to any of those places," she responded. Her eyes were on him but she didn't seem focused. "I'll probably just go stay with Toya for a week or so. She has her own family, so I'm not even sure about that."

King was listening to her but he had an idea of his own. He picked up his cell phone and dialed Harmony's number.

"Hello?" she answered.

"Hey," he replied.

"Where the fuck you been at all night?" she growled. Then she asked, "You heard somebody killed your cousin?" He removed the phone from his ear at the sound of her loudness.

"I got into a fight at the club last night and ended up at the hospital. I'll be home shortly," he told her. "Hey, I was calling you because something happened to Delishus' apartment and she can't go there right now. Do you mind if she comes to stay with us for a couple days?" King asked.

"Motherfucker it ain't April, but you got to be the biggest damn fool to ask me some dumb ass shit like that! Get off my damn phone, playing with me! You bring that bitch into my house and I will kill her and yo' ass!" Harmony threatened, hanging up the phone in his face. He looked over at Delishus and didn't have to tell her how that call went.

"It's okay. You are not my guardian. I am a big girl and I can handle being on my own. I'll call my people to go stay with one of them. I have two brothers here and my parents live in Decatur. Don't worry about me. I'll just have some family go by there to get a few things for me until I can get it all moved out," she stated.

"I really want to be where you are. I don't want anything to happen to you. After finding out that Harmony isn't pregnant by me, I have made my decision to be with you. Will you have me as your man, Delishus?" King asked. Her eyes lit up like a Christmas tree.

"Of course I will!" she said, rushing over to hug him.

They embraced and kissed each other. "And you got to know that I ain't letting you out of my sight from here on out. I got a couple dollars stashed up, we can get a hotel room until we find us a place to stay."

That statement alone just made her feel so good she couldn't even hold back her tears. When she started crying in his arms, he just wrapped her up tighter and caressed her, giving her the feeling of something real. King was indeed hung up on Delishus and definitely wanted to be with her. On the other hand, not only did she want King, in her heart she needed him and wasn't about to let him get away. Delishus felt as if a thousand pounds of weights had been lifted up off her shoulders.

CHAPTER 21

She lifted her head and glanced around the room. The dungeon that she was in smelled like urine and death and was dreadfully cold. Looking over to her left, she saw a woman shackled in chains. Not knowing if she was dead or alive, Delishus jumped at the sight of her. That of course brought to her attention that she herself was shackled to a wall like a slave.

She thought about the two dudes that had those young girls held against their will in Ohio a couple years ago. The young woman was almost similar to her size as she too was thick and could almost be a long lost sister with the same facial features.

"Miss? Can you tell me where we are?" Delishus asked nervously. The woman turned to her, showing her scared and battered face. She finally realized that she had seen the woman before however, she couldn't recall where at.

"Mmmmm," the woman moaned with tight lips.

"Shhhh...." she responded, slowly shaking her head.

"Where are we at? Do you know how you got here?"

Delishus questioned. Forget being quiet, she wanted answers and somebody was going to give them to her.

"Be quiet, or else he will punish you. I don't know where we are at. Hell, I don't even know how long I've been down here. All I know is that Germane got us." the woman advised with more alertness.

"Germane? That's right. I was with him last time I checked we were supposed to be going to a club to dance. Did he do this to you? Oh my goodness! If you don't know how long you've been down here, chances are that I'm stuck here with you!" Delishus' heart begins to tighten and she felt a cold aura wash all over her.

"He doesn't like confrontations. He wants you to accept what he offers and do what he says. I met him a while ago at the club I worked at. Don't judge me, but I'm an exotic dancer. My name is Chaunee but I go by Candy."

"As in a stripper?" Delishus asked, raising an eyebrow.

She never met a woman of Chaunee's size performing in such an occupation. She'd heard stories about it, but this was actually her first time meeting one.

"What? Why you say it like that? I take my profession seriously and prefer to be called an exotic dancer. I ain't stripping much but I can dance while lighting the room on fire," Chaunee advised.

"No, it's not that. I just find it fascinating that a woman big like us, or you rather, would be confident enough to take on that profession. No disrespect though. I understand women have to do what they need to do to make money. You said you met Germane at the club?" Delishus responded.

"Yeah, we went out on a couple dates, but he began to get real impatient with me not wanting to take him serious. He was too clingy and controlling for me though. I was used to having my freedom and enjoyed being able to live the lifestyle I had freely until he came along. We dated for about two months. Then when I tried to cut him *off, he just continued to come by the club causing a scene. The owner had him prohibited from coming there and I even filed a restraining order against him."*

"Damn, are you for real?"

"Yes. I should warn you that he is abusive and finds it amusing to torture women. If I ever refused to eat or declined on pleasing him sexually, he would beat me. Do you see that belt over there?" Chaunee said, taking Delishus attention to look across the room. She nodded once she saw it. *"That's his favorite weapon. He whooped my ass yesterday like I stole something. Hit me all in the face and didn't care that I was screaming to the top of my lungs. I just hope next time I disobey or do something he doesn't like, that he doesn't kill me."*

"The fuck! How do we get out of here? Have you ever escaped? We have to get out of here. Help me with these chains. Feel like I am in a bad episode of Roots," Delishus stated.

"It's no use. I have tried everything and still haven't managed to get out. What day was it yesterday, since you say you were out then?" Chaunee asked.

"It's July... can't remember the exact date though," Delishus advised. The look on Chaunee's face confirmed that wasn't good news. "Why you look so sad?"

"Because when I last saw day light it was cold as hell outside. In fact, it was close to Valentine's Day because I wanted to end things before then with Germane. I didn't want any obligation of being his for that day. Valentine's Day should be shared with someone you love, not someone you are forcing yourself to like," Chaunee explained. She began crying and got quiet once they heard the doorknob turn. "Shit! He's coming..." she said, adjusting herself back up to the wall. Delishus could smell the fear reeking from Chaunee all the way on the other side of the room.

"Hello loves," Germane said, making his grand entrance as if he was a waiter coming through at a five star restaurant. He had two trays in his hand. "How are those wounds healing up Candy? Hope I didn't hurt you too bad, sorry if I get a little out of control. But you know daddy doesn't like to spank you unless you deserve it right? Do you forgive me?" he asked her. He slid the tray in front of her exposing the rat poison sitting on top of the soup.

"Hell no, motherfucker! Fuck you! I would rather be dead than to keep living in this hellhole! You have her now, so let me go!" Chaunee advised.

"Hey!" Delishus interjected, getting offended at how quickly Chaunee turned on her.

"Now Candy, I take real good care of you so that you have a roof over your head and food to eat. But I figured you would say something like that. Here, eat some soup, it will make your wish come true."

Delishus couldn't see it but Chaunee could. She spit in his face, letting him know that if she did die, it would be on her own terms. Delishus stiffened at the site of what went on between them and worried for Chaunee. Especially after knowing how long he'd had her hidden from the world. Who knew his purpose and what he planned for the two of them. Germane wiped the spit from his face, looked at it on his fingers and let a half grin creep across his face.

"Okay, I see we have to do this the hard way." He picked up the spoon, scooped up some of the soup and brought it to Chaunee's mouth. She shook her head "no" and closed her lips tight. He got tired of her fight, seeing that whenever he attempted to force her to eat the portion, she turned and rejected it. Germane grabbed her cheeks and squeezed them until she couldn't stand the pain. Chaunee opened her mouth to scream, giving him the chance to jam the spoon in her mouth. Once it was inside, he covered her mouth preventing her from spitting it out. She gagged and choked hard resulting in a cough so

viciously that she couldn't help but swallow some of the soup. She spit up some of it causing it to get on his hand.

"Ewww! You nasty bitch! I said swallow it!" he told her, removing his hand in disgust. Delishus sat there watching and thinking how easily she could be in Chaunee's shoes.

"You bastard!" she said once she finally caught her breath. "What did I ever do to you? Why are you doing this to me?" she cried. Chaunee could feel the ingested poison slipping down into her stomach. She knew it was only a matter of time before it ate up her insides and did its job.

"Rat poison? You poisoned her? Why? I don't understand what's going on here? Germane please just let both of us go free! We promise not to tell anyone," she pleaded. She sat and watched as Chaunee puked and threw up more than just the portion he had fed her. Her body jerked and she clutched her stomach from the pain.

Her phone chimed to Beyoncé's "Petition" snapping her out of a horrible dream and bringing her back to reality. After being held captive, she continued to have nightmares and dreams of Germane. She pictured his face just as clear as day. She prayed everyday that he wouldn't come back to kill her or harm anyone in the midst of trying to get to her. She didn't know what the dream meant but, considering that she was staying up in a hotel for now, she knew her days of being locked away in her apartment were over. She called the police that same night and filed a restraining order, took out a warrant and whatever else she could do against Germane. She also had the police search her apartment to show her landlord proof of needing to break her lease. They found traces of blood from two people of whom she knew to be King's and Germane's. Delishus looked at her phone noticing that it was her brother calling yet again.

"Hey Tee," she answered.

"Baby sis, what's the deal? I saw you called and I got your messages while I was at work. I'm on break and I can come to the hospital if you need me to. Are you okay?" he asked.

"I'm fine, but I'm at a hotel. Can you and Shane go to my apartment and move some of my things to storage? My landlord has another apartment complex down from your house and he says he can get me moved in but it will take two weeks. I'll pay for the storage, but I'm at the Marriott downtown until then," Delishus explained to him.

Tee was the eldest of the three and considered Delishus to be the baby, even though she was the middle child.

"Of course love. I'll tell my boss I have an emergency and get on it right away. Shane's lazy ass should be home right now, so it won't take us long to move the few pieces of furniture that you have. Call the storage and let me know which one it is. Do you have any idea where this fuck nigga is at?" he asked.

"That's what I'm afraid of. I have no clue where he is, or if he knows where I'm at. I'm scared, bruh. I have never experienced this before," she admitted.

"Don't worry. Me and the boys will clear out the apartment, if he comes there he'll regret it. I tell you that much. Send me a pic of him just in case. I want to put up a picture of this bastard so that they can catch him. I don't want my little sis worried about being in the city. This is your hometown and you should be able to go as you please without dealing with fuck shit like this. I also told you 'bout dealing with these clown as niggas round here. How long you two been talkin' anyway?" Tee said.

"Only for a few months. If I saw any signs of this earlier, I would have backed off a long time ago. I have a friend who is helping me right now. He saved me, and I thank God that he cared enough to come by the apartment to look for me when I hadn't been able to communicate with anyone," she told him as she looked out of the window.

"Yeah, well tell your friend I thank him and I'll see you soon, okay? Don't forget to send me the picture. I'll call you to keep you updated," Tee said, hanging up the phone. She turned around after ending her call with her brother and went to the bed where King was laying and watching her. She walked over to the bed and stood next to him. He reached out for her and she climbed in and laid on top of him. They kissed one another softly and she felt so safe with King.

"My brother said 'thank you'," she whispered.

He didn't say anything, but gave a brief nod of the head. His hands were all over her until they just laid in one another arms. Then he whispered, "I love you, Shawty."

She smiled.

"You better." Then she added, "Cause I definitely love you." They cradled in one another's arms. She fell asleep though King was wide-awake, holding her. He knew she was somewhat traumatized and to a certain extent, he was too. He still had a lot on his plate and he still wasn't clear on the murders that he'd committed. He was worried about his monkey ass baby mama too. She was too cut throat to even be around and her mother was just as bad. They said the fruit didn't fall to far from the tree and that statement was true. However, at the end of the day he was still King and he had the woman he loved right by his side. He rubbed her stomach in small circles, thinking about their baby that was on the way. King wasn't about to be broke and bringing another child into the world. But for the meantime, he was good and blessed, and he had his BBW.

To be continued...